Orlando in the Cities

Optimist

Orlando in the Cities

First published in *A Quantum City* by Birkhäuser in 2015

ISBN 978-1-63821-999-6

Optimist Books by Optimist Creations
optimistcreations.com

Contents

Preface

In the summer of 2014 I received an unusual request: could I write a story that took place in four different cities, in four different eras, told in four different literary styles.

The story was to form the core of an anthology called *A Quantum City* which was being compiled on the 'generic city' by Diana Alvarez-Marin and Miro Roman who were then both PhD students at Professor Ludger Hovestadt's chair for Computer Aided Architectural Design—since renamed chair for Digital Architectonics—at the Swiss Federal Institute of Technology, ETH Zürich. He and Vera Bühlmann, who is now professor for Architecture Theory and Philosophy of Technics at the University of Technology Vienna (TU Wien), were the Editors and they had decided that this "colossal work" and "love letter to the city," as the publisher was later to describe it, needed one, and only one, bespoke text to tie together the hundreds of fragments of all kinds from Homer to Machiavelli, from Goethe to Gainsbourg, from The Old Testament to Stanley Kubrick, that had been assembled and structured into four principal parts. Not an essay or an academic treatise, but a fictional narrative that would portray The City through the ages.

During our first discussions we agreed that the four cities and their eras should be Florence during the Renaissance, Elizabethan London, Paris at the time of the French Revolution and Vienna at the turn of the 20th century. To complete the arc, I then added onto this a Prologue in Alexandria at the end of the Classical Greek period and an Epilogue that takes us to the emblematic city of the second half of the 20th century, New York.

What I also proposed early on and what was readily embraced was the idea that, if we were going to have a storyline through the ages in different locations, it might be interesting to attach this to one character who travels through time without ageing and without particularly noting that peculiar circumstance, a bit like Orlando, the eponymous 'hero' then 'heroine' of Virginia Woolf's creation. In fact, why don't we take the character of Orlando and expand his, then her, story into the past and the future with a touchpoint in the middle: when we are on the frozen river Thames in London.

Whence stems *Orlando in the Cities – A Playful Odyssey Through 2,500 Years of Western Civilisation.* It is an homage, of course, to the 'original' Orlando, as much as it is a celebration of language and of the city. In its original context—*A Quantum City*—the four parts were given titles that appertain to the anthology as a whole. With the text here standing on its own, these may seem less obviously relevant, but I very much like them for being evocative and abstract at the same time and so I have ‘borrowed’ them and retained them with a couple of minor adjustments for this edition. Similarly, I have kept the epigraph that prominently features on the first page of the ‘big book’: it is, surely, just as apposite for this small book too.

I wholeheartedly recommend *A Quantum City:* if you ever wanted to own a book that doesn’t so much tell as show you how we got to be where we are today as a society of societies and a communion of cultures, this gives you as comprehensive and wide a perspective as you could wish for. But ever since it was published I felt it would perhaps be attractive also to make the *Orlando in the Cities* story available as a self-contained, separate edition, so that anyone who enjoys this kind of character and language driven narrative may have easy and compact access to it, which is why I am releasing it now in paperback and as an ebook.

In doing so, I owe an immense debt of gratitude to Ludger Hovestadt and Vera Bühlmann, and indeed to Diana Alvarez-Marin and Miro Roman, without whose vision and inspiration this short but in its own way epic story would not exist.

Sebastian Michael
London, January 2021

We are all migrants
native to the universe

Orlando in the Cities

Sebastian Michael

Preamble

Orlando—figment of the imagination, ideal and idol and fallible in every way conceivable but flawless in the eye of the beholder—is given to the world perfectly formed by the gods, themselves constructs of the human endeavour to conquer the unknowable and unknown.

Timeless, ageless, and deriving immense powers mostly from an indomitable spirit paired with an enquiring mind, Orlando is all human, all humanity, all humility and all pride: an articulation of the embodied consciousness we may call the experience of being alive.

Not good or bad, nor beyond the pale is Orlando, Orlando is wonder and discovery and surprise; and strife for self and self-knowledge and hunger for connections that mean something; and need for identity, desire for the loss of self and urge for survival; and yearning for the tender release that is death and fear of the violent crash into the absence of life that is dying. And aching for a place in history and undoing that history bit by bit. And invention, creation, as much as destruction. And cruelty and kindness and the duality of all things polar and their fusion. And the idea of being itself.

(Never even mind religion and statehood and status and tribe and the blood ties that bind and sin and redemption or even forgiveness.)

Orlando is all made up which is why Orlando is real, and Orlando, of course, is ancient as much as Orlando is new.

Orlando is charged by the gods—subject as they are to their own whims and fancies and with wisdom endowed no more and no less than we can conceive—to embark on a quest to The City.

And so, as we go to The City, our protagonist shall be Orlando...

Prologue

Alexandria

320 BCE

Grant, Muse, that these verses may in simple truth
bear witness to the man (then woman, then
hermaphrodite) whom since the dawn of time
the gods, and mortals too, have called Orlando:
through the ages, yet un-ageing, bold, adventurous,
cast of an ilk of ceaseless curiosity,
journeys Orlando in the Cities –
let this be his (then her, then their) tale, told
or sung: begin upon the seas off Egypt...

Behold how through the haze on the horizon
shimmer turrets white, gold and pale ochre;
Lighthouse, Fortress, Temple and Museum:
new-built Alexandria, Great Alexander's
monument to his own glory, yes, but more
the lasting glory of mankind: trade, commerce,
the exchange of stuffs and wares; and above all
pursuit of knowledge, learning and ideas.

*

But a slither in the distance is the coast
as on a steady breeze the wide-hulled ship
sails south-south-east; a friendly school of dolphins
playing escort, clicking joyful greetings
to her precious passenger: Orlando.
Never has his heart yet beaten faster,
have his eyes gazed harder at the glorious sight,
his nostrils smelt the scent of sea salt keener,
his hands, fine-fingered, tighter clasped a rope,
nor have his curls danced lighter, has his skin
more giddy felt the air's caress than now
with the approaching prospect of the city:
planned, built and peopled surely to perfection,
jewel of Greek provenance on Egypt's soil,
in Hellas' crown its youngest, finest pearl.

The ship glides into harbour with the sun
low in the orange-purple sky, Orlando
poised to jump ashore, eager to gather
what he may: symbols, writings, artefacts,
medallions, coins; anything portable,
anything proof, if such exists, of what,
if anything, makes cities good, for thus
the mighty gods themselves have set his task.
No task, no challenge, such as this could be
accepted lightly, and nor could it fail
to fuel zeal in someone like Orlando:
he is to travel Greece in search of proof
to settle a dispute which, days ago,

broke out between the gods. (That he should now
be just about to land in Egypt is, in turn,
their doing, but of that twist more anon:
we mortals are but playthings of the gods!)

On that day, Mount Olympos was aflare
with fury: Hera, in a huff over some
minor matter had admonished fair Athena;
she quipped back, and before long an argument,
involving several other gods, ensued,
which rapidly grew loud and would, no doubt,
have turned tumultuous too if thunderous Zeus
had deigned to get involved; but he did not.
(At least not while he tried to have a nap...)
The quarrel soon abated and the gods,
four of them left, Apollo and sweet Eros
besides Hera and Athena, now discussed,
rather than argued, which of the great cities
each patroned merited the epithet
of 'perfect' or 'complete' or, by deduction,
'unimprovable'; what Thomas More, much later,
failed to call 'Eutopia': a good place, where
naught is amiss; to Mount Olymp itself
for mortals an equivalent. Each god
extolled their city's virtues: queen Hera
spoke of Argos, Perseus' birthplace, and its
gentle, peaceful people whose pristine and
modest dwellings cluster at the foot of the
magnificent acropolis, harmonious,
exquisitely arranged and amply furnished

with necessities from mountains, fields and sea:
what more could from a city mortal souls desire?
"What more?" incensed, cried Ares, god of war,
and entered straight a plea for Sparta, home
of warriors. "No gardens, no fine buildings,
no temple of great note: these are peripherals!
Sparta, more than any place, has discipline,
valour and strength: the art of the Agoge!"
Apollo was appalled: "What Spartans do
in their Laconic ways is the antithesis
of art and culture: how can you begin to think
of 'city' and not think its streets, its courts,
its alleyways, its amphitheatre, its games;
not think its dramas and its comedies,
its music, poetry; and to protect it all
a sturdy wall with seven gates: think 'city' then,
think Thebes: that is a place fit for the gods."

Athena sat in silence for a while.
Then she stood, calm, gracefully and in a
quiet, gentle voice declared: "You make me laugh."
A pleasant titter rippled from her lips
and down towards the earth as a soft whiff
of fragrant mountain air that freshens the stale heat
of noon; but this was followed by a frown –
a measured mien of mild concern betokening
a worry for her fellow gods: "But please
be serious: a city perfect in both shape
and population; ideally positioned,
with monuments that will be celebrated

for as long as humans live and far beyond;
in art, in sculpture, in democracy
and in philosophy, in military strength
and in the soft delights of love, be they
in passion felt or quietly in friendship kept;
a city where the merchants and the warriors,
the scholars and the politicians and the poets
and the athletes and the women and the slaves
all thrive, each in their rightful way, in harmony:
that is a city worthy of a goddess' name;
a name which I, Athena, lend with pride and joy
most willingly to Athens, in this noble world
of cities, queen." With that she sat and silence
settled over Mount Olympos once again.

But for a short while, to be sure: for a
hiatus barely long enough for all the gods
to catch their breath, before, aroused from blissful
midday slumber, thundered Zeus: "What is it
with you children, wife, wherefore this waffle?"
The gods explained. Upon which Hermes, drawn
into the hall by all the noise and Zeus's roar
offered a way to solve the matter, once,
if not perhaps for all... – "Why not," swift-witted
and wing-footed Hermes made propose, "dispatch
into the world in search of evidence
a mortal who has never been to any city
and has never seen its sights or heard its sounds
nor yet inhaled its fragrances nor met
its people, who has lived in plain simplicity

upon a hill, and yet whose spirit, mind and soul
are lively, quick and eager; who may learn and then
impart to you such wisdom as he finds;
whose unencumbered, fresh and hungry heart,
in short, will, without prejudice, present
to you the perfect city on a plate."

There was another stillness in the hall, until:
"Whom do you have in mind?" Athena asked,
and not without some slight suspicion, knowing
the wily ways of her half-brother well, who
with a winsome smile replied: "Orlando."
"He in Crete?" There was, in all of Greece, but one
Orlando: Hera's question was superfluous;
Orlando (he in Crete) was well known to the gods
for was he not—no god or mortal could be sure—
the offspring of Dionysus and a young
shepherdess? What could be known for certain
was that he'd been found, and taken in and
cared for by the man he called his father
and his buxom wife, and that of all the boys
(six brothers and three sisters in their brood)
Orlando was by far the fairest and most gentle,
most refined, most clever and most curious,
though also, if here truth be told and so it be,
when tending sheep the laziest. So prone
to getting lost in thought and in the process
losing some, or—as on one occasion—all,
his father's sheep was young Orlando that
his father (and his brothers, though less kindly, too)

indulged the boy, allowing him to mainly lie
among the olive groves or vineyards and compose
sweet songs and poems that he would perform
at early even time for their diversion.
All the gods, including Thunderthrower Zeus,
were smitten with Orlando and would make
small gestures of affection secretly devised
to favour him among his village clan, and
none therefore were doubtful now that Hermes too
had plucked the youth from his obscurity
to feed (and still) a lingering desire,
but the gods, as is their wont, will make allowance
for such feeblenesses as among them
they are only too familiar with, and so
none hesitated nor did anyone object,
but readily did they endorse the stratagem
wing-sandalled Hermes had devised, and swiftly now
at once did Hermes swoop to Crete to find
Orlando on the hillside underneath
his favourite olive tree, as usual, sound asleep.

Alighting by Orlando's feet, the messenger
did pause and gaze, enchanted, at this face
that, carefree in repose, and, with the speckled
sunshine through the leaves playing an undulating
patterned game of light and shadow on his cheeks,
seemed made of nacre, marvellous and fragile
and mysteriously soft yet to the touch,
and on Orlando's forehead Hermes laid his wand
to gently waken him. This did not work:

too deep in slumber had Orlando sunk;
lost, dreaming of a lover's warm embrace,
in tender fantasies, which partly now came true
as Hermes cupped his hand around his neck
and drew him near to kiss him on his lips,
which brought Orlando back from dreamland in a flash.

"I have," spoke Hermes, as they both reclined
(following a short, impassioned tussle
that was certainly no dream, Orlando thought,
and yet too dreamlike to be taken quite as real)
"a task for you, which we, the gods, are certain you,
Orlando, are ideally placed to make your own."
Orlando, still aglow, glanced as if through
the messenger god's face and, mesmerised,
replied, "I will." – "You have not heard yet what it is."
"I will do anything you, in the name of gods
or mortals or such creatures as you may invoke,
command me to." – "But I do not command,"
protested Hermes, "I invite you, if you choose,
to acquiesce." – "I acquiesce wholeheartedly!"
exclaimed Orlando, flung his arms around
the god once more and kissed him many dozen times:
"What is it you would have me do?" – Hermes demurred:
"It is not me that you will please, nor shall I be
recipient of your service: but the gods
on whose behalf I speak, bid you set forth
and journey to the cities of our lands
to find what makes the fairest fair, the strongest strong,
the most agreeable and pleasant so,

and bring back evidence that may, at last,
settle the question vexing them: who holds
as patron the epitome of cities."

At this he rose and, looking deep into
Orlando's eyes, gave him one more kiss on the lips
and, "you will have guidance, counsel and good speed,"
he said, before he took his air-bound leave.
Orlando, in a daze, sighed, "well, I may,
if all this is to come to pass, make my way
down from this hill now to Heraklion, where
cousin Lefteris' friend's father owns a ship
that sets off frequently from Crete to Athens:
the only other place of which I know
they call it 'polis'; thence, I have no doubt
I shall find other 'poleis' that serve to prove
or disprove any argument the gods dispute
and if it pleases Hermes that I please them so,
it pleases me to be their eyes and ears
and gatherer of evidence (if such exists)."
And without bye or leave or much ado
thus did Orlando; which is how it came to pass
that within days he found himself at sea,
embarked upon a voyage of discovery
to Athens. Athens. – Not Alexandria.

Earth-shaker and god of the seas Poseidon,
reeling from his loss of Athens to Athena
(though many centuries by now had passed),
acquainted by Nerites of Athena's boast,

and young Orlando's quest and voyage thither,
threw his trident in a rage down to the ground
and caused the sea off Milos to rebel and swell
three fathoms high, letting the skipper of
Orlando's ship fear for his and his cargo's life
and sail as safely as he could around the isle,
then between Milos and Sifnos bear due east,
where gusts inflated by Poseidon's ire
propelled them further down and further still:
no end in sight there seemed, for day and night
and day again, and night, until, at last,
with the sun rising for the third time since
they'd spotted land, some calmer waters gave
the fragile vessel a long longed-for welcome
to plain sailing and respite. Orlando,
who had never been at sea, had turned in hue
as pale as the thin hazy clouds that lingered
in the distance between sea and sky, and
with supplies of food and wine now far too low
to risk returning to their erstwhile course
the skipper offered an alternative
as thrilling, he assured his fare, as Athens:
throbbing, thrusting, thriving Alexandria.

Orlando did not mind. Out on the deck again
and gently rocking on the soothing waves
he reasoned that a detour of this kind
was, like as not, the gods' intent, and who,
he thought, was he to ponder on their will.
"The gods," Orlando mused, though to himself,

"in Alexandria will make it known to me
what in their name I might be doing there,"
and off he dozed. – The gods were not so sure.
For Alexandria was new. And none of them
did know it well, nor had the citizens
of Alexandria yet cared to call upon
a deity as their patron; no, their sole intent,
it seemed, was at this point to grow, and grow
their city did: with every day more people
came to stay, eager to build and keen to trade,
prepared to dare, to put at stake
their livelihood, if not their dreamed-of future
in the new place named after the emperor
who brought the world he made his own to them.
And did it come: from far afield as China,
India and Arabia did wares arrive:
spices, gems, dried herbs and fruits, and ivory,
skins and silks and drapes and rugs and mosaics
and plants and medicines and, prized above all:
knowledge. Knowledge as had not been known before:
not only were new thoughts here thought – new ways
of thinking thoughts, ideas of what ideas might be
and records of such thoughts as had been thought
now found their home in Alexandria:
a hub of trade and commerce that became
a haven for enquiry and reason.

Orlando, who had never been to school,
but whose bright mind was ready soon to burst
with curiosity, had scarce set foot

on firm Egyptian soil before he found himself
in the Mouseion's hallowed halls where not the gods
but all the muses were revered, and within days
illiterate country boy of yore, Orlando
found a teacher like none other in Euclid
and formed a college with some peers who much like he
had never once before soaked so in knowledge;
Orlando felt his mission was already done.
Here, surely, was the city of all cities
a place where people relished *everything!*
What multitudes he witnessed coming, going
sometimes standing in a spot, in conversation,
and what conversations he so overheard
and soon felt bold enough to have himself:
he would, thought young Orlando, simply stay
here for some time and learn and practise what he learnt
and then return and take with him some papyrus
and write down—soon he would be able to!—
everything he'd seen and heard and done.
Beyond that, he was now convinced, need be no search:
perfect, indeed, was Alexandria.

At this point, Chronos entered in the fray.
Chronos has no time for trivial pursuits
such as the games his fellow deities
enjoy to play so frequently on humans;
he has no need for tributes and vain offerings,
for temples or for shrines, or cities given
to his name; Chronos is the god of time,
and time is endless for as long as there is time;

and there is nothing anyone can do to hasten
or to slow time in its pace, and Chronos knows
that every moment present next becomes
a moment past, and that the past is but
a future presently unmade by time, and time
itself is but the way we witness our decay,
to be reshaped as something else or maybe
something similar, in constant cycles,
ever-growing, ever more enlarged, until
time ceases to exist and we are gone.
Love may not be time's fool, but time is no-one's fool
and, irked by the bickering of his cousin gods,
Chronos decided here to intervene.
"Minions," he cried, mostly to himself, for they,
as usual, cared not and paid no heed to him,
"what is perfection in the now when time
yet writes the histories, yet moves the skies,
yet makes a future certain though it be unknown,
yet turns each fleeting moment to a lasting past,
each monument to rubble, every pantheon
to dust: speak you of the city of all cities
and think not of time and cities yet to come?
Oh vanity, oh unsupportable conceit!
You may be gods and think yourselves beyond
the ravages and promises of time,
but what you speak of is not so: your witness
shall bear witness to this too and travel
far beyond the realms alone of land and sea,"
and for his purpose called upon swift Hermes,
just as the other gods had done before.

He to Orlando and with Hypnos' help (the
limitations of his own caduceus known)
sent him to gentle sleep, but not before
reminding him that time was short (the opposite
would prove the case, but this Hermes did not relay)
and coaxing him, with promises of wonders,
wisdoms and of winsome folk more worthy
of his admiration than what he found here,
upon a merchant vessel, large and tall.

And thus Orlando, worldly now, acquainted
with philosophy and algebra, and art
and poetry and history; conversant
in both Greek and Latin, and in Arabic:
a young man now of learning and some wealth
(Tyche, unsurprisingly, had smiled on him)
did sail across the sea of Mid-Terrania
bound, in deepest slumber, for Byzantium.

(This time, none other than Dionysus,
god of ritual and fertility,
religious ecstasy, the theatre,
harvest, winemaking and indeed of wine
in all its wondrous workings was to blame—
if 'blame' can be a word employed to name
the impact of the gods on our fate—
that the strong ship in which Orlando sailed
did veer off course again and make headway
elsewhere: the seas were calm, the winds
unfurious but fair; it was the captain

at the helm who savoured all the pleasures
that Orlando's rumoured father stood for
just too much to keep a steady hand and
soon landed, haphazardly, in Italy...)

I

Welcome to the City

Florence

1504

When in the twilight of an autumn morning,
Slumped on the benches of a horse-drawn coach,
Inside my heart each mile of distance scorning,

I weary from my travels did approach
The city they had praised in songs euphoric—
Which fear and doubt let on my mind encroach,

As I could not imagine their rhetòric:
A city so magnificent and grand,
Her classic styles, Corinthian and Doric,

Her marbles sculpted by great master hand—
I raised my head and saw how yonder place,
Embedded in the hills rose from the land

In harmony and with the utmost grace,
Blood new refreshed rushed from my happy heart
And joy re-found wrote laugh lines on my face.

Once more with thrill tingled my every part,
As it had done when centuries ago
I first encountered Alexandria's art;

But even those who had described her so,
Since on Italian shores my foot I set,
Could not upon her so much worth bestow

As did her splendour on her own beget:
This Florence was in truth of all the gems
Most precious in the city-carcanet.

Now knew I whence anticipation stems!

But even so was I not well prepared
For the exquisite Heaven through whose gate
Our humble carriage passed, where I but stared

And breathless, toneless, voiceless thanked my fate
For taking me to such a place as this,
And took my leave now from my travel mate,

Who had, together with a friend of his
Since Empoli been at my side and talked
Of Florence and the now impending bliss.

Now was I on my own again and walked
Towards the Duomo and its Piazza, where
Men with an air of great importance stalked

Among the people who would gather there
To worship their one god and to behold
The beauty of the buildings in the square.

I could no longer blame the ones who'd told
Me of these things in hyperbolic praise,
Nor can a man of mind and reason scold

The fathers of this city if they raise
Their heads with pride when thus about they go:
There is no simple, modest turn of phrase

Encompasses the wonders here on show.

I knew within an hour of my stay
That thus the perfect city must be built
And nothing hence would from this place me sway.

Nor would I be restrained by fear or guilt:
I would procure plans, drawings, models, maps,
Beg, blag, cajole, steal, rob, charm, what thou wilt,

Then take them back to Hermes and perhaps
Produce some writings of mine own to stress
That though there may have been in time a lapse

This treasure, this discovery will redress
Whatever failing any god may find
In any of their cities and impress

Upon them the ingeniousness of mind
That here was on display, alive, at work,
Unparalleled in spirit, skill and kind.

Therefore by the Palazzo did I lurk,
Where those high men had gone with purposed stride,
Thus leading me by fortune-fated quirk

Where power and the powerful reside,
And not for long did I there have to wait
Until among some townsfolk I could hide

And slip into the den of this proud lion straight,
In search of any library or vault
As I in Alexandria had seen of late,

Wherefrom I was convinced I could not fault
But bring sequestered on me in some way
A multitude of objects to exalt

(And if by stealth) the Florentine array.

A council on that day had been convened
At which the Elders and the Great and Good
Debated where in preference they deemed

In an ideal case a new statue stood.
Hewn from a local marble seventeen feet high,
And of commensurately heavy weight, it would

Be nigh impossible to lift, or try—
With pulleys, ropes, contraptions or machines,
As ordinarily one would—to fly

And raise the object above ground; such means
Were all discussed, examined and dismissed:
"If it into thc wall bumps or carccns,

Or falls or tilts or, once up there, should list
And drop, then will this masterpiece be lost:
The only way that it securely may exist

Is on the ground, and at much lower cost!"
Thus went the argument both to and fro,
As councillors and dignitaries crossed

Their words, that it was thus, and thus not so:
"The statue was conceived to tower high
above by Master Michelangelo!"

"That may be so," a bearded man would sigh,
"But it will not withstand the heavy strain.
This marble will not keep, again say I:

We need to shelter it from hail and rain."
And back and forth until it was agreed

The protestations were to be in vain:

This David, as they called him, was indeed
To stand within the Piazza on the ground,
Where children and old women pigeons feed,

By the Palazzo's entrance, firm and sound.

The council now arose and from his chair
The bearded man, a twinkle in his eye,
Gave me a wink, I could in turn but stare

As he deliberately passed me by;
I had behind a drape thought me unseen
And, now discovered, wondered how and why

The old man, having found me, did not mean
To apprehend or even question me;
Yet from his gentle mischief did I glean

A call to follow him, and quickly he
Into an antechamber peeled away,
So only I from where I stood could see.

I made to join with him without delay,
And by some secret shortcut doors and stairs
He through a warren led our getaway,

Along the corridors where the affairs

Of state in reverent silence were pursued,
Midst grandeur to which none I knew compares,

And up a narrow staircase where we viewed,
From high upon a shallow balcony,
Which from the graceful tower did protrude,

The glory of the city's tapestry.
Here did he speak at last: "Welcome to Florence!
Who are you? And why so stealthily

Do you your presence here with us commence?
You obviously hail from foreign lands:
What brings you here and why this shy pretence?"

I felt a tremble through me, and my hands
Began to shake; I mumbled, ill at ease:
"I am Orlando, my mind understands

No more than my heart knows why the gods please
To send me here, yet have I just one quest:
To find the perfect cities and in these

To gather evidence; and with my best
Intentions, though my means must be judged ill,
Sought from this building lasting proof to wrest."

The old man laughed and did not stop until
His breath ran out and even then he grinned,
Then chuckled, then guffawed out loud, but still

Spoke not, till, mocking, he intoned: "You sinned
Unpardonably!" Then he burst out once again
And teased me further: "We are most chagrined."

Now was I perplexed, and it was then
That someone else out on the terrace crept:
The quietest, most serious of men,

Who had in council his own counsel kept;
He gave me a suspicious smile and said:
"Don Leonardo, it is time you stepped

Down and rejoined the others who are led
To banquet by the Cardinal; his Grace
Is troubled that you from his party fled."

"Don Niccolò," the old man with grave face
Replied, "I follow; and I bring this lad
Whom as a guest I heartily embrace."

And like a friend of many years who had
Been absent and now happily returned,
He introduced me, saying: "We are glad

To have Orlando who did lately learn
Of our city and who comes to seek
The very truth for which our own hearts burn.

As you can tell at once: Orlando's Greek."

*

It was not long before I was installed
As an assistant, model, help and friend
At this da Vinci's, Leonardo called,

And by and by I tried to comprehend
How one mind of such genius as his
Can every thing he wants his passion lend.

And yet in Florence there was more than this:
In every church, in every other square,
In workshops, studios, academies

Did artists their identity declare
And unmistakably impress upon the world
Works that their signature alone could bear.

All this was new: what here so fast unfurled
Was a fresh way of thinking yet again,
As if the minds like petals had been curled

In tiny cusps through long dark night, but when
The morning sun awakes them from their sleep,
These dazzling flowers in their beauty then

Begin to blossom for the world to keep
The fruit that follows at the harvest time,
And summer has returned to winter deep.

Here did the bells of reason newly chime,
Here did enquiry into truth abide,

And truth itself was given a new rhyme.

Though men like Leonardo still must hide
Some of their studies in the cloak of night,
Their curiosity broke open wide

The pyxis that kept knowledge from their sight
And put it into the realm of men,
To be examined in the clearest light.

Now for the first time did I see the ken
Of simple but compelling human form
Delighted in and on display again,

Since it in Ancient Greece had been the norm:
But now perspective and anatomy
And a view of the Cosmos built a storm

That changed art, science and astronomy
In the most powerful, enduring way;
Geography, too, and philosophy

Spoke in a new voice with new things to say.
But nothing, not even da Vinci's hand
So absolutely took my breath away

As when at last I in the square saw stand
That David by young Michelangelo:
Never before had anything so grand

So unbelievably alive and so
Exquisite in shape, texture, poise and grace
On this wide world been made and put on show:

Even the art I had seen face-to-face
In Alexandria, or in Heraklion
Could not match this, although this showed its trace

Back to the Greek Antique, whose pantheon
Had to innumerable works of art
Been inspiration, muse and champion:

Now did the Florentines usurp their part.

In politics too were there shifting sands:
Florence was not a quiet, peaceful town,
Nor were the neighbour cities, states and lands

United under one commanding crown.
As a republic Florence long had thrived
And lately lifted from Piero the gown

Of a *de-facto* ruler that derived
From centuries of influence and might
On which his clan, the Medici, survived.

Now ousted and in exile out of sight,
Piero lo Sfortunato was he called;
But there was one man who from Piero's plight

Took inspiration and in secret scrawled
Down everything he heard said, or saw done
And later wrote a work that both appalled

And thrilled in equal measure anyone
Who read it, because here was put in print
Advice on power, and how power's won

Not by divine authority or dint
Of moral rectitude, or even force,
But by the devilishly cunning glint

Of dry intelligence and a divorce
From sentimental values, bad or good,
And cold manoeuvring without remorse

Against whomever in the way of power stood.

I had met him on the day I first arrived,
When down from the Palazzo's tower he
Had summoned Leonardo and contrived

That at the banquet he sat next to me,
Where, charming and intelligent, he sought
To understand from me what strategy

I was employing, and what spark of thought
Had got me to the heart of his domain,
When others' efforts never came to aught.

(His questioning to me did seem in vain,
As to the gods beholden I still felt
And therefore could not argue or explain.)

Since then I at da Vinci's house had dwelt,
And he on several occasions drew
Some sketches of me where I stood or knelt,

Or lay or jumped or sometimes even flew,
In an imaginary flying thing,
That he, nor I, nor no-one else yet knew

Would ever to the world much purpose bring;
And so my face in drawings did occur
That to attention among those might spring

Who to da Vinci's labours would defer,
And soon one lady's lover did request
That for a portrait it was I not her

Who to the master lent my face and chest,
And so protect his anonymity
While giving him, "in all the world the best

Of likenesses and some proximity
To her own features, though the artist would
Imbue his work with femininity."

So he declared, and so da Vinci could
Not but obey, for he was high of rank,

And so it was that I of womanhood

Became an icon, and I him must thank
That now a thought began to germinate
From which my mind new inspiration drank,

Wherefore a knowing smile would permeate
The many drawings Leonardo made
From which the lady's painting to create.

Thus months passed, and the year began to fade.

I soon sensed time was nearing that I bade
My host and also mentor now farewell
And, knowing he would find another aid,

Of my intention started out to tell,
Upon which Leonardo sat me down
And from a chest whose treasures I knew well

Removed a book, some scrolls, and with a frown
Reminded me of what I had declared
That day when I had first arrived in town:

"You came to us unspoilt, unwise, unscared,
And you delighted me with your bold youth;
And what you lacked for being unprepared,

You made up with your deep desire for truth.

So if you go, take from me these three things
That will assist you in your future sleuth:

This is a book, a Letter, and it brings
News from a New World, newly told of late
By a man born in Florence whose name rings

Across the world, and it will resonate
Beyond our days: Amerigo Vespucci.
Mark that the impact of his work is great

In exploration and cartography,
Therefore read this and take this map with you,
And these sheets of our own topography.

Take drawings of our buildings, yes, but do
Not think that here is where the city ends:
With us modernity begins and through

People like him, and you, the road that bends
Beyond our own horizon has a goal –
Not to be reached; but as your own way wends

Into the future, drawing from the soul
Of every age that you are party to,
You by degrees can make your story whole,

Which is the best thing anyone can do."

*

This said, he guided me across the floor,
My few belongings and his timeless gift
Came in a leather bag and at the door

His boy, Salai, now offered me a lift,
"At least as far as to the city gate,"
And with a firm embrace we parted swift.

While Salai drove, my mind did ruminate
Upon these men, these works, this panoply
Of genius: how it did celebrate

The human spirit, how the canopy
Of heaven in this city was a tent
In which to house all of humanity.

Then, at the city limit, where I sent
Il Salaino back to the great man,
I still had on my face that smile and went

Along the road towards where it began
Back to Livorno and its port, but lo!,
A carriage stopped and offered me Milan,

Wherefore Milan was where I thought to go.

II

We Are the World

London

March 1603, January 1608

I.i

Enter The Queen supported by Attendants, Sir Robert Cecil.

QUEEN
Succession, succession. Succession indeed.
All I ever hear of is succession:
Has ever month, or week, or day gone by
Without the word succession being whispered
In my ear, louder than clarions of war?
Will it not cease? Not now, in my demise?
Will ever yet my soul hear mournful cries:
Where, where, Regina, where now is thy heir?
I have no heir but that my spirit live!
Triumphant in adversity and scorn

Do I deliver this realm to her new dawn;
And my successor? Must I name him, must I
Now in words defile myself when in my mind
And in my body I so long held firm? –
But look, here comes Orlando, pray withdraw;
I'll this vexation ponder yet anon.

SIR ROBERT
Ma'am. I'll on the hour return.

Exeunt Sir Robert and Attendants.

I.ii

Enter Orlando.

ORLANDO Majesty!

QUEEN
Oh apple of mine eye, sweet sight Orlando.
My politicians seek to wear me down
With the same question that has haunted me
All of my life. Who shall succeed me, who?
I am not sorry that there is no heir.
Would I could choose one, pick him from the crowd:
Wouldst thou, if I so bade thee, be a king?
Oh please say no. The king's lot is a bane,
And thou hast lives to live, maidens to pluck:
Fresh flowers from the gardens of their youth,
And youths to lead astray in gallantry... –
Be thou not one who would be king or queen,

Be thou Orlando even as thou art:
Simple and pure, and maddeningly fair!

ORLANDO
I assure you Ma'am, that I would not be king,
Not for a thousand crowns, not for the sceptre
That commands the world and all the stars;
Not for the kisses, promises and lies
Of all the lovers ever known to woo.

QUEEN
What would you be, Orlando, if you could?

ORLANDO
Why, I could be Orlando, if I should.

QUEEN
I warrant that you should, if you but would.

ORLANDO
Aye so, but aren't we merely players, all?

QUEEN
Who shall I tell them then should play my part?

ORLANDO
No-one can play your part, Ma'am, it will die
When you your costume and your wig remove;
And it will never so be played again,
But for the boys and youths who on the stages
Of the theatres will take it on in time

To act your part as you: Elizabeth
Gloriana, Good Queen Bess of England.

QUEEN
They want the King of Scotland to come here
And reign in both our kingdoms' name as one.

ORLANDO
Does this displease you?

QUEEN It unnerves my heart
And makes my mind numb with anxiety.

ORLANDO
How so?

QUEEN Orlando, my sweet boy, I am
A figurehead, an icon, an ideal;
I am what England wants to see in me
And what it yearns for, deep inside:
Untainted grace, and steely will united
In one person: fragile china figurine;
Warrior too. Virgin, mother, queen and whore.
Oh look not so: I am not scandal, no!
I am but fantasy of fornication;
Therefore am I safe and unimpeachable.
The King of Scotland is a nobody.
How then will my people, will my England
Forgive me for not giving them a king?
Will not for victory I be remembered
Over Spain, for saving our religion,

Not for loving our people above all,
But for abandoning them to a Scot?
Will I have failed, Orlando, dismally?

ORLANDO

Worry not so, my queen, Your Majesty.
The English are at heart rumbustious
And gregarious, it's true, they do distrust
A man of intellect and quiet study,
But have they not seen monarchs come and go,
And somehow thrived? Your work is done. You leave
Them stronger than they ever were before:
Could, in our time, a woman have prevailed
The way that you have, had she borne a child?
Had she unto a husband given in?
Think what a husband is unto his wife:
A lord and master. Could the Queen of England
Have given England this, her all, and still
Been mother to an heir, wife to a prince:
Faithful and true not to her country first
But first obedient to her royal man?
Maybe the day will come, I trust it may,
When this would seem no more impossible
Than for a king to force upon his people
Terror, famine, deprivation, strife and war
And still be called a saviour of sorts.
I say, Your Majesty, be free of guilt,
Of pain, of passion and of purpose now.
Allow these days to pass like so much mist
Over the parkland of a morn in March,
Before the sun on the horizon does appear,

And, with its first rays, rise and quietly give way
To a new day whose course cannot be known
Nor yet its pattern seen. Have done, my queen
Let go and be content that England
Will go on. Let England choose her queen or king:
The people get the monarch they deserve.

QUEEN
The way you speak belies your years, Orlando.
Walk with me, let us into the gardens:
Though the air be chill, yet is it fresh and clean;
These walls have heard too much, the tapestries
Are stale with sorrow, anguish and despair.
The vows that have been broken here, the words unsaid
With false betrayal evermore to stain
The fabric of the state: the weight, the weight
Of it, layer upon burdened layer... –
Sir Robert will return, let us escape,
An hour among the ancient trees; but no:
Speak of the devil. How now, Sir Robert?
This was not an hour's peace!

I.iii

Enter Sir Robert.

SIR ROBERT   Your Majesty,
I fear me these long talks will wear you down.

QUEEN
Have you no fear, Sir, I will hold my head

Aloft a few more days. The Ides of March
Are not upon us yet. We'll for a walk abroad;
Dispatch to Scotland thus: "So trust I that you
Will not doubt but that your last letters are
So acceptably taken as my thanks
Cannot be lacking for the same, but yield them
To you, thus, in grateful sort." – He shall be king
But let for now the missive be in code.

Exeunt.

II.i

Enter Courtiers, Orlando.

COURTIER 1
You do yourself injustice, Lord Orlando!

COURTIER 2
False modesty does not become you, Sir...

COURTIER 3
Quite so!

ORLANDO Pernicious flattery. I am
Of all the men upon the frozen river
Clumsiest by far, I wave my arms about
Like one possessed, I nearly fall, then fall,
Then get up on my feet, then fall again;
My knees are bruised, my wrist is nearly broken,
And my limbs feel heavy as if made of lead:

Pray, let us rest and drink to our host
The King!

COURTIERS The King!

ORLANDO And his good health!

COURTIERS Hip hip
Hooray! Hip hip hooray! Hip hip hooray!

All but Orlando sit and recline.

ORLANDO
But what is that? What does mine eye espy?

COURTIER 3
And yet he will not sit. – Allow yourself
Some respite from the ice, Sir, soothe your legs!

COURTIER 2
(A fine pair though they are, they do appear
To both of them yield into two left feet...)

ORLANDO
What is this vision on the ice swoops by?
He has the grace and stature of a youth
But yet when she moves close she has the figure
Of a lady. Oh let this thing be real!
Let this not be a figment of my mind!

COURTIER 1
My Lords, the King!

They rise.

COURTIER 2 The Earl of Somerset
As ever by his side. His favourite...

COURTIER 3 ...is young.

COURTIER 2
Young and well-favoured too. But then Scots are.

ORLANDO
Pray silence, lovebirds, here the lady comes!

II.ii

Enter Sasha.

SASHA
Messieurs.

ORLANDO Mademoiselle.

SASHA Je suis enchantée.

ORLANDO
Vous n'êtes-pas Française.

SASHA Mais non. Je suis Russe.

ORLANDO
Добро пожаловать в Лондон.

SASHA
спасибо.

ORLANDO
Lord Orlando, please call me Orlando.

SASHA
Princess Marousha Stanislovska Dagmar
Natasha Iliana Romanovitch:
Do, by all means, Orlando, call me Sasha.

ORLANDO
May I show you the ice sculptures, Sasha?

Exeunt Orlando and Sasha.

II.iii

COURTIER 1
He is engaged to be married, is he not.

COURTIER 2
Alas.

COURTIER 1
I could swear I saw a spark there of love.

COURTIER 2
Or lust.

COURTIER 3
Well, the Lady Margaret O'Brien O'Dare O'Reilly

Tyrconnel, on her left hand's second finger, wears his sapphire.

COURTIER 2

A splendid sapphire, his.

COURTIER 1

What grace. What courtesy, all of a sudden. I could swear I never saw him hand a lady to her sledge before.

COURTIER 2

Not to her sledge.

COURTIER 3

No, it is true: never has woman from young Lord Orlando received so much attention as the Princess Sasha.

COURTIER 2

Nor no man.

COURTIER 1

I wonder will the King be pleased.

COURTIER 2

Or Lady Margaret.

COURTIER 3

Or Prince Romanovitch, if there is one...

Exeunt.

II.iv

Enter Orlando, Sasha.

ORLANDO

Now can you see how far we've come away:
The tents and stalls, marquees and canopies
In size are turned to toys in which the king
And all his entourage are making sport
Of the great chill. Soon will the sun go down
Beyond the palace, and the light will fade,
And all the lanterns and the fires that burn
Will turn the ice into a magic crystal maze.
And when the moon that full now rises yon
His glacial glance upon the snow doth lend
The world to us will all seem but a dream:
Then promise me that you will never part!

SASHA

I will not part as long as winter's hand
Holds fast onto the ship wherein I came
And keeps her anchored at the river's mouth
Gripped dead in stillness on the frozen waves.

ORLANDO

But then? What when the ice melts and lets go
Will you to Moscow then embark again?
Stay here, or else, allow me that with you
I turn my back on country, courtiers, king:
Become a Russian, just for you. Like you
A Muscovite. And we can move to the

Siberian steppes: I hear they are like this
The whole year round, a frozen desert land
Where the warm-hearted live in isolation
From the follies of the world, in solitude;
Thus shall we, with wolves and bears our company,
Make our own home as fugitives from court,
From politics, from flattery and favour,
And lead our simple lives with simple pleasures
In simple love and simple harmony.

SASHA
Oh sweet Orlando, would it could be so!

ORLANDO
O, but it can. I have no ties that bind me
Nor have you, or have you? Is there on the ice
Among the party, on your ship, or hidden
Somewhere, or, worse still, plain on display
In the emissary's train a lord who claims
To call you his? Then let him get away!
Let him with the Ambassador to Russia
Whilst we into the English countryside
To build a nest for just the two of us.

SASHA
Kiss me, Orlando. Let this hour pass
In dreamlike wonder: how clear your eyes beguile,
How hot your hands in mine my heart impel!
Feel my cheek as I feel yours, this night is ours
Alone and if all other nights belong to
Princes, kings and queens and their ambassadors,

Here can we say, and now, for one brief moment,
"This is us, let all that matters be our love."

They kiss, embrace.

ORLANDO

But see that woman struggling with her pail:
Old, frail and decrepit. – All ends in death.
Has she not danced and skated on the ice
Fond in her lover's arms and wished herself
Nowhere so dear as where right then she swept,
Her feet above the ground, her head in heaven,
Thinking the world's sphere her little oyster.
Look at her now. Slow. Limp. Unsteady. Cold.
Arthritic fingers clasped around the handle,
Her wobbly gait with every timid step
Wasting the stinking brew she calls a stew.
All ends in death. And death comes far too slowly.
They that say for them it comes too fast all lie:
It can't come soon enough. And yet at times
I feel perhaps death never comes at all.

Sasha kisses him.

SASHA

A smile again at last. And they say we
In Russia are too prone to melancholy.

ORLANDO

Sasha, we shall fly. I'll make arrangements:
All will be thought of, nothing will go wrong.
The next dark night, a week or two weeks hence,

When once again the moon has waned enough
And turned from silvery medal back to sickle,
When a few clouds his little light obscure,
And darkness cloaks the streets and alleyways,
Then to the port of London and to sea:
We'll to your motherland, I will not leave you!
Together we will make our way and we'll outlive
The dredges of our time, we'll be as young,
As beautiful, and as in love as we are now.
Say yes! The words I'll whisper in your ear
Shall be *"jour de ma vie!"* – when you hear this
Just nod to let me know you've understood,
And at the stroke of midnight at Blackfriars
(I'll draw a map with most precise instructions)
Will I have horses ready, and a ship
With passage paid to Antwerp and then thence
To Copenhagen and St Petersburg.
All ends in death, dear Sasha, but today
We live and this day of my life is you!

Exeunt.

III.i

Enter William Shakespeare, Ben Jonson.

JONSON
That will be it then, for another score years or so.

SHAKESPEARE
Who's to say? What if our winters are just getting colder?

JONSON

Nonsense, our winters are not getting colder, what do you think this is? An age of ice?

SHAKESPEARE

Why not exactly that, an Ice Age: gradually, year on year the winters getting colder, the ice lasting longer, until it all freezes over, *perennially*.

JONSON

Perennially? You do make words your slaves, Will.

SHAKESPEARE

I'm just saying: we don't know.

JONSON

Well what we do know is it's pouring down with rain and any man still on the river will have to count himself lucky if he makes it to its bank in time.

SHAKESPEARE

Will there be drownings?

JONSON

I fear me there will.

SHAKESPEARE

There will be flooding?

JONSON

Aye, I believe so.

SHAKESPEARE
Will there be looting too, and misery and murder?

JONSON
There will most likely be some murder, and a fair amount of mayhem too.

SHAKESPEARE
You've seen all this, and witnessed it before?

JONSON
I have, I was thirteen when it last happened.

SHAKESPEARE
That is not one score years ago.

JONSON
Give or take a few...

SHAKESPEARE
Well, be that as it may. It only confirms what I've known all along: this town is no place for tragedy.

JONSON
If drownings, looting, misery and murder don't make a place one fit for tragedy, what does?

SHAKESPEARE
It's, as you say—I do, for once, agree with you—all but mayhem. Mayhem is not tragedy. Nor is it comedy. It's just unwarranted upheaval. Which is why this town is

not a place for comedy either.

JONSON

What is this a place for, in your esteemed opinion?

SHAKESPEARE

It is a place for irony, which I am useless at. A constant knowing contradiction within everything.

JONSON

But you do contradiction well: your villains are charming, your lovers heroic, your youths are maidens, and your kings of late have turned to fools...

SHAKESPEARE

That is not irony, my friend, that is human nature. I can do human nature, of course I can, I see it all about.

JONSON

What, then, is a place for tragedy?

SHAKESPEARE

Anywhere. Anywhere but London. London is too aloof, too knowing, too ...sophisticated.

JONSON

And what is that supposed to mean?

SHAKESPEARE

Impure, adulterated: suffused with self-awareness. For tragedy to be tragic, it has to happen where the heart rules and the nerve is raw. Imagine a man steps into the Mermaid Tavern here tonight and says: "My love is drowned." We see no tragedy in that. Nor is it comic. Yet we smile—tinged with a hint of sympathy perhaps—because it would be deeply ironic.

JONSON

Don't use 'sophisticated' in your plays, Will. Nor 'ironic' neither. They sound foul on the ear.

SHAKESPEARE

I have no intention to. If I wrote the way I speak, people would never believe me, nor would anyone listen to me, and why should they: I am a poet, not a pamphleteer.

JONSON

So anywhere but London for tragedy. And for comedy, Verona?

SHAKESPEARE

All Italy for comedy. Italy is inherently comical. But then it is inherently tragic too: the two go hand in hand; it is inherently theatrical. Pure emotions, grand gestures, loud voices, hearts worn straight upon their sleeves where you can see them, hear them pound.

JONSON

This is all the most ardent nonsense. London is as good as any place for comedy, tragedy or history, you've never even been to Italy: it is not possible to sail by sea from Milan to Verona, they are landlocked towns!

SHAKESPEARE
I hear they have canals.

JONSON
Canals?

SHAKESPEARE
It would be possible to sail on a canal, would it not, they do in Venice...

JONSON
How would you know there is a canal that links Milan with Verona? Your geography is trivial and unsound. And that's what irks me so: you are slapdash and cavalier in all you do.

SHAKESPEARE
It's *poetry!* Who cares? Who cares if Milan has a port or Verona a harbour. I may give Bohemia a coastline if I want: it is poetic to sail, prosaic to ride, and so I'll put on a boat whomsoever I choose and let them sail whithersoever the wind of my fancy may blow!

III.ii

Enter Orlando.

ORLANDO
Milan has a canal. A grand canal.
As grand as Venice. Though I doubt it reaches
To Verona. Nor does that in Venice.

It ends, like all, in death. The sea is death.
And my love did drown in the rain tonight:
Call it ironic, poets, if you please.

JONSON
Capital fellow! Are you drunk?

SHAKESPEARE
A bit the worse for wear, perhaps, the hours that were small are waxing, after all...

ORLANDO
She said she would: she said she'd come. She lied.

JONSON
Ah wenches. Don't they ever...

SHAKESPEARE
She did not drown?

ORLANDO
Drown. Lie. Not come at the appointed hour:
What's the difference. All ends in death. I'm gone.

SHAKESPEARE
Stay, friend! Have one more ale with us!

ORLANDO
Who art thou, that thou callst me friend so soon?
We have not met: I might yet be thy foe!

SHAKESPEARE

Not so, I think. This is my young friend and, dare I say, young rival Mr Jonson, but as a friend of mine you too may call him Ben. And I am William Shakespeare, call me Will.

ORLANDO

I have heard of you! You are a friend indeed!
You wrote a play that sometime I did see.
More than a poet, you're a dramatist!

JONSON

Being a dramatist counts for more than being a poet? How things change...

ORLANDO

Are you a dramatist? I know you not.
You may be a friend of William Shakespeare's,
But you are not his match. I will not have it.

SHAKESPEARE

Drown your sorrow, friend. I may yet have a poem for you.

ORLANDO

Not now. My heart cannot sustain the pain
Of poetry. I saw her ship. It sailed.
It sailed without me but with her on board.
And that's the worst of it: I saw it sail.
We were together to elope to Russia.
To the wilderness that is Siberia.

Instead my heart is broken with no hope
That she return or I to her may go:
What heart is it that has no hope at all?
So long as I did not behold the flag
On the Ambassador's vessel growing faint
So long could I hold hope that she might come.
But she did not. Now all is lost. Oh woe
Is me, that held her in my arms and danced
Upon the ice with her, looked in her eyes
And felt the tendernesses of her lips:
They all are nought. Now all is lost. And all
All ends in dreadful, lonely, coldheart death.
So no: no poems for me now, no song!
Let me in silence suffer as I now not
Drown my sorrow, but myself in sorrow drown:
I'm gone. Bid you goodnight, poets and all.

SHAKESPEARE

Wait, not so fast! We need to know your name, your calling on this earth: how do you do, what is your life?

ORLANDO

What is my life, aye what. What have I done.
Failed, I have. Loved I have, and lost, not once
But the innumerable times of ever:
Ever have I loved yet ever have I lost.
Is't better to have loved and lost than never
To have loved at all? You tell me: poets
That you are, but then again, who knows, perhaps
This is too soon. Will you remember me?
I am Orlando. I have lived... – that's it!

I have been tasked; I have a mission to fulfil:
That is my life, to garner evidence
Of perfect cities. You are well met both!

JONSON
We are? All of a sudden?

ORLANDO
You and your play, The Dream, Midsummer Night:

SHAKESPEARE
What of it?

ORLANDO
Set in Athens. I was bound for Athens once
But didn't make it: last place I remember
Is Milan, though I spent no more time there
Than a man might need to fall asleep, and then
The next thing that I know is I am here,
A favourite of the Queen. The Old Queen Bess,
Before she died. She was too old for me
And yet I loved her, and she dearly me.
But that was then and this is now, and James
Was making sport upon the ice and then
The ice was gone. And gone was Sasha, so
Show me London. Take me to her monuments.
St Paul's and the Exchange, the Tower, surely,
And I know your theatre, it is a gem!
But show me everything there is to know;
Give me your city, gents (you are no gents, though
Are you, you are poets! Be that as it may...)

I would scarce find myself here if not London
Were of all the cities in the world the one
The gods should know about: show me your town!

SHAKESPEARE
A place the gods should know about.

JONSON
That's rich.

SHAKESPEARE
Are you sure you are not a bit of a poet yourself, Orlando? The gods: the Romans had their gods, so did the Greeks.

ORLANDO
Then you know my meaning man: let us go forth!

JONSON
Orlando, mark me, London is a monster.

SHAKESPEARE
Aye. And ravenous at that.

JONSON
And sickly too. How many times since you've been here, Will, have we had the plague?

SHAKESPEARE
Half a dozen times or more.

JONSON

And dangerous. You're not a papist, I take it, but still. Spies, everywhere, I warrant I thought for a moment you yourself might be a spy, but spies who raise their porter to the ale are rare: they thrive not in this world, as they get quarrelsome and have themselves stabbed at the tavern or out in the alleyway, we hear too much and know too little of it, but you know not what your fellow man may think or tell. Therefore take heed. And as for monuments?

SHAKESPEARE

There are none.

JONSON

None of note, for sure. The Exchange: it is a market place. The Tower: it's a prison. St Paul's: a church. Which city in the world has not a market place, a prison and a church?

SHAKESPEARE

The theatre: yes. Go to the theatre. And what find you at the theatre? Why: people and their stories. Characters.

JONSON

That is what you get in London town. The gods, were you to bring them here, would find no place of marble, brick or wood that they would wish to make their home, but they'd meet murderers who smile, diseased seductresses, and venerated fools, scorned wise men, and benighted elders, and much youthful wit; apart from which an ever-heaving hive of busy-ness with traders, merchants, bankers, seafarers and opportunist fortune seekers. Yes: if you want the world in one place, come to London. My friend Will here thinks it's not a place for tragedy, or comedy at that, and who knows, maybe it is not, but one thing is for certain: it's the place for people.

ORLANDO
Ah people. Yes, I remember them too.

JONSON
He's in a funny mood, this one.

SHAKESPEARE
Can you blame him: he is lovelorn!

JONSON
Sir, Orlando: what say you, we will take you to a play tomorrow!

ORLANDO
I'll think on it. My mood is fading fast.
Perhaps the spirit of the ale is waning.
What of your poetry: you say you have some?

SHAKESPEARE
This:

He produces a piece of paper, ink and a pen. Writes from memory; hands the writing over to Orlando who reads.

ORLANDO Oh my!...

SHAKESPEARE

You're one who's loved and lost: I know your heart.

ORLANDO

I know not what to say.

SHAKESPEARE

Then stay in silence. It is golden.

ORLANDO

Thank you: let me but thank you...

SHAKESPEARE

Shhh.

ORLANDO

But...

SHAKESPEARE

No thanks. No payment. No reward. No protestations. Something will come of this. So worry not: your face, to have seen it; your voice, to have heard it; your heart, to have recognised and known it: everything will yield; you will in many shapes and forms live in somebody's words, wherefore no words are necessary now. Trust that it be so: the rest is silence.

JONSON

You're quoting yourself, Will, no wonder your career is going downhill: You take yourself too seriously!...

SHAKESPEARE
Come to the theatre at Blackfriars tomorrow. The King's Men will be giving a play. It isn't one of mine: it will be none too serious.

ORLANDO
I will come to the theatre tomorrow.
I will see any play a playwright wrote
That lives and breathes in London, for it is
A brave new world that has such people in it
As they write here, for they do write them all!
Goodnight to both of you, I feel myself
Already bound to you Will Shakespeare:
I'll remember you, fear not. And if the world
In its incessant quest for novelty
Distraction, entertainment, mirth and sport
Forgets about you: I'll remember you,
This sonnet. Are there any more like this?

SHAKESPEARE
Many.

ORLANDO I'll keep this closer to my breast
Than any thing I ever held, my own
Weak efforts not excluded. But do not so:
Find a way, Will, any conduit that
Gets them off your chest. For there they are not safe!
Allow somebody who has access to them
To retrieve and publish them and do it soon,
Before doubt and the melancholy yen
For self destruction, the grave's growing pull,

Before forgetfulness and wanton age
In its obstreperous senility
Prevent you from it. Do it now: the lover
You immortalise with your delicious words
Will keep them still. Someone you know will know him,
Someone close, but not too close to him, someone
Who owes him nothing and who isn't owed;
Does such a man exist, or woman?

SHAKESPEARE Yes.

ORLANDO
Then bid him do it. If, for your allegiance
And your love, and your devotion to this day,
You cannot bring yourself to publish them,
Then let that person be the vent through which
Your heart is finally set free and given
Over for the world to keep. I'll now be off
But see you both tomorrow at the play!

Exit Orlando.

III.iii

SHAKESPEARE
Wrote I not in a play the name Orlando?...

JONSON
So you did.

SHAKESPEARE I don't remember what it was.

JONSON
No, nor me neither.

SHAKESPEARE Nor will anyone:
It was but a diversion for its day...

Exeunt.

III

Parades

Paris

1789

Chapter 1 — In which Orlando, mysteriously yet unspectacularly turned woman, sets out for Moscow, but ends up in Paris instead.

I deem it, Esteemed Reader, superfluous to necessity at this juncture to acquaint you in exacting detail with the occurrences, the unfoldings, indeed the happenstance surrounding the events that—astonishing to the mind that is inclined toward reason though they may seem—are certain to have befallen, enveloped or, is it fair to say, been visited upon, Orlando, at some point subsequent to Princess Sasha's ship sliding off the receding ice from the frozen river Thames into a rain-sodden estuary and after his encounter with two ale-touting poets at the Mermaid Tavern in the relative vicinity of Blackfriars. Other chroniclers will have had cause greater, and means more powerful, than mine to relate with some authority how he—and of Orlando at that time still being a 'he' there could be little doubt, and certainly none reasonable—had spurned the advances of the taller-than-usual Archduchess Harriet Griselda of Finster-Ahorn and Scand-op-Boom (in the Romanian territory) and had had himself posted by the King as Ambassador Extraordinary to Constantinople, where, having practised diplomacy with admirable alacrity, and after laying on some splendid entertainments, he fell into an inexplicable, or at any rate unexplained, trance lasting seven days; and how finally, and in spite of the vain muffling attempts by the Ladies of Purity, Chastity and Modesty (though this may be interpreted in an allegorical sense) Orlando woke up to an equally allegorical trumpet blast of *'TRUTH!',* rose, stood upright in complete nakedness and—the trumpets still pealing *'truth! truth!'*—appeared before himself, before the world, and thus before us, as a woman.

It is thanks to the skills and the unwavering adherence to Truth of said chroniclers that we know how Lady Orlando, in character and disposition unaltered, in her memory—perhaps some little haziness, some dimmed clarity permitting—unchanged, had spent time with the gipsies on a mountain before returning back, at last, to England, there to take care, before anything else, of some matters pertaining to her person and the legality of said person's irrefutably newly defined standing in the world.

*

Accepting then that this was so and not otherwise and allowing therefore no argument or disputation for the time-being over the whys and wherefores of Lady Orlando's new state of being, I take it upon myself, with your permission, Dear Reader, to regale you instead with the events those former ones ensuing, which, I warrant, shall reveal themselves to be of no less importance in our heroine's life's proceedings than many others, even though, admittedly, few changes and alterations would ever have been, nor ever prove to be, of a similarly profound and incisive nature as those experienced by her in Constantinople and mentioned afore.

Was it coincidence, or was it fate, or was it an underlying wistful memory, or was it none of the above, or all of the above combined, that prompted Orlando to yearn more than for any place for Moscow, as she stood by the Oak Tree—subject of her poem long in the composing—and beheld how the land surrounding her lay covered in snow, how the trees stood barren and bare against the dark grey low-lying clouds and how the gloomy skies so adorned seemed to suggest nothing so much as endings, and how endings were in the distant recess of her mind forever associated with death? Never had she been to Russia, nor had she felt in a long time this desire for distance, for winter, for melancholy—or was it merely a still lingering longing for Sasha? Which, Orlando couldn't tell—and not in recent months or years had she felt overcome so with the caressing ache of despair as now, but certain she felt, the youthful verses she'd carried so long and so fond so close to her bosom now resonating in fragments through her newly-troubled mind, that Moscow was where she needed to go, and no sooner had this realisation lodged itself in her mind than the decision was made: some post, some purpose, some position in Russia would surely be hers for the asking, provided she asked the right person, and Orlando had never been, nor was she now going to be, one not to know whom to ask! Down she strode, wrapped in her cloak, a walking staff in her hand, relishing the air which struck her chin hard and fresh now with the clean chill edge of resolution: Moscow it would be, she would arrive there in April, maybe in time, just, for Easter.

Straight for London did Orlando make, after an evening's preparations, deliberations and also one or two minor prevarications: 'Is it wanton to do so?' she asked herself, pacing two steps south-south-west in the library, where she was wont to go when her mind felt unease, 'when there is clearly so much here to look after, so much business to attend to; when so many matters of weight and import are to be seen to about the house with its three hundred and sixty-five bedrooms, its kitchens and drawing rooms, its attics and cellars, its outhouses and stables, with all the land about it, the orchards and the fields, and the *Oak Tree?'* she pondered. *'But alack! What are they to me!'* next she exclaimed, with an inflexion that suggested more protestation than query, 'when I have no meaning here and no purpose, other than to sit out my time? What, indeed, is my time?' she wondered to herself, as she stood and paused briefly, facing her gamine figure in the looking glass, before pacing back two steps north-north-east to the window overlooking the frozen paths that led to the frozen pond where the half-frozen ducks skidded on the ice comically without any such intention, and in doing so stoked that glint of a memory once remembered, that warmth of a love once embraced and then discarded—no not discarded! Had torn away from her! That's what it had been, had it not: a love torn away from her, back then when she was a man?—and still she stood again, now resolute and determined. Putting herself up at her townhouse for just a few days, which readily turned into three weeks, Orlando made enquiries, procured provisions, arranged documents for travel, and, having paid no less than three visits to the still very young Prime Minister (barely four years older than she was herself now), and dined with him and his friend twice (the second time, it should perhaps be noted, on the part of the two politicians, somewhat reluctantly), a commission, passage and lodgings were finally in place, and nothing stood in the way of Orlando setting off to Moscow, representing, once more, the crown, although this time, on account of her gender, in an unofficial capacity, of which neither the Prime Minister nor his friend was able to be entirely certain exactly what it was; but they were glad, her undisputed charms and delightful conversation notwithstanding, to be rid of her with little prospect of her inviting herself round to the 'vast, awkward house' at Downing Street for further dinners, at least for the time-being.

"It is not," said William Wilberforce over port in the withdrawing room, "entirely clear to me what a woman, with no vote in her own country, little if any education (or at any rate none evidenced and proven) and a personal history that may be declared dubious if one were charitably inclined, somewhat suspect if one were less so, may hope to achieve with the Russians; but then none of our most skilled emissaries have ever, to the best of my knowledge, achieved anything with the Russians either, and so why should we not, in the spirit of that greater parity between the sexes that we strive to explain to our nation as something to be aspired to, and in service of equanimity at our own dining table, appoint ourselves a lady Envoy, Special as inevitably she would have to be. The Russians, I daresay, will be enthralled to her: her French, it appears, is impeccable."

"Quite so," replied William Pitt (who was, among the Williams the elder, but certainly among the Pitts the Younger), and proceeded to refill their glasses (the butler for the evening having been stood down so they might enjoy some little privacy, at last).

On the eve of her departure, Orlando went for a stroll in St James's to clear, we may assume, her mind and to reflect, it seems likely, on the immense undertaking that spread out before her, as vast, she felt, as the Siberian steppes themselves (although she had no intention, on this occasion, to venture east of Moscow at all). The weather was unusually clement for the time of year—it was still only late February—and it would be many years, she surmised, before she would set foot on England again. This did not discomfit her unduly, nor did it make her happy; rather, she felt the time had come to embolden herself and take her destiny, such as it was, into her own hands and find, if not meaning as such, and not, perhaps, even purpose, then at the very least an application of herself to something meaningful, something purposeful, although what this might be she felt she could not know; what she knew in her heart was that she would find it as long as she did not allow herself to be thrown off course again, as she sensed she had done on too many occasions before.

Pleased with the reassuring certainty this thought furnished her mind withal, Orlando sat down on a bench overlooking the water in the edifying twilight of a portentous day nearing its close, and that mind was now at considerable ease, her face in a calm, almost serene repose, with her gloved hands gently crossed over the walking stick resting on her knees, when a young gentleman just about her age, or maybe two or three years younger still, cutting an unreasonably dashing figure for this time of year in a Royal Navy uniform professing a rank higher than the soft down on his cheeks and upper lip would appear to permit, stopped in his tracks as he walked by, turned to face her directly, stood upright as a pillar, took a brief but courteous bow, banged his heels—somewhat sharply, Orlando thought—together and spake, in a voice much more in keeping with his years than his rank:

"Madam, may I ask the provenance of your cane?"

Orlando looked down at her hands and gave the Malacca just the slightest of twists.

"I brought it home from Constantinople; it was a gift..."

At that her eyes lost focus for a brief moment, as the memory in her mind gained sharpness in turn:

"...that was left me, by a friend."

"It is a fine piece of wood," said the young man, with not a hint of irony, bowed again and seemed about to turn, when Orlando explained:

"It belonged to Charles Wootton Fitzpaine, Ambassador to Penang at the time, he had it made especially, with wood from the Calamus; would you like to try it?"

The young officer beamed like a child at the suggestion, and as Orlando got up and handed him the stick, she noticed that he was just about an inch shorter than she. He bowed his brief, almost curt, bow again and exercised the Malacca up and down the pathway with such vigour, such joy, that Orlando couldn't help falling quite hopelessly in love with him, in the way that one can only fall when there are less than twenty-four hours in which to do so. Orlando felt the pang in her heart that announced this passion, recognised it, knew how perfectly impossible and hopeless a sensation it was, how preciously unwelcome, how infuriatingly delicious, how insanely inconvenient and yet how apt, and, with a world-weary sigh descended back on her bench to watch him turn on his heels, twirl the stick, and strut like a boy, the dimples in his cheeks irresistibly calling. Once again he halted and the dimples vanished:

"Why are you sad?" he enquired with innocence as

light as a fresh summer breeze and concern as grave as the seas on which he must sail.

"Please," said Orlando, "accept it from me as something to remember me by." She rose again, she curtsied, she walked away. She got no further than seven paces before he had overtaken her and stood in front of her once again:

"I know not your name."

"Will you walk me to your ship, Captain?"

"I am a Master and Commander only, my lady, and my ship lies in Gravesend, some twenty-odd miles hence..."

"Then walk me to my house, my Master and Commander, it stands in Mayfair, but eight hundred yards from here."

At this point in our narration, Most Valued Reader, it behoves us well to let the drape of night descend on Lady Orlando and her gentleman naval officer on their enjoined own, for it is not done to pry into the affairs of the newly acquainted when the circumstances demand that they be so readily befriended lest the too small window of opportunity should close, and that—should their hearts be so inclined—they become enamoured ere they must part, or never taste the delights of love at all. Suffice it then for us to know that morning came in its wanton glory, and neither Orlando nor her young lover were willing just yet to disentwine. Luncheon passed, then tea time and supper, but still did no-one emerge from the house, other than the housekeeper who was sent for fresh fruit near sundown. Meantime, also at Gravesend, and no more than a half dozen piers downstream of the naval vessel from which the officer had taken his temporary leave, a captain of a merchant brig bound for the Baltic, who had been told to expect a passenger on official duty, finding that this passenger remained absent and made no sign of boarding any time soon, and knowing that he was no more able to stay his departure than to stem the tide, was left with no choice but to lift anchor without her, and so for the second time a ship set sail for St Petersburg that Orlando should have been on, but wasn't, only this time amorousness was what kept her, rather than propelling him thither.

A second night passed much in the vein of the first, and both Orlando and the young officer would have happily had it turn into a third, and even a fourth, had not the call of duty rung out overbearingly loud in the officer's ear, and unlike Orlando, he was in no position to let his ship sail without him unless he was to face the harshest of consequences.

"Stow me away on her, withersoever she sail," whispered Orlando in that same ear, and the tickle of her voice and the warmth of her breath softened the rude noise that duty had made, and the sailor took Orlando as well as some of her cases—albeit far fewer than originally intended for Moscow, including one or two of her hats, but really none of her furs—and brought them onboard, straight into his cabin past the gawp and cat whistle of some crew and a highly raised eyebrow accompanied by an admiring smile from his captain. He, in turn, was something of a rogue and rascal of the old school and, once on the North Sea, had no compunction to intersect the course of a merchant ship and send his own gang onboard to press some of her topmen and boatswains into service, substituting them for his least capable crew. Orlando was aghast: she had been at sea before and she had heard sailors' tales of hardship and woe, but she knew from the faces of the dejected men who appeared now on board like slaves to a galleon that she must leave before her sense of justice and indignation made her speak up and cause a commotion or, worse, a mutiny, for while she could not brook the treatment of the men she witnessed, neither could she reconcile with her conscience bringing the young gentleman who had taken her on at some risk to himself into trouble, and so before the ropes were untied, Orlando, with only her purse of gold on her, and wearing her most comfortable hat, jumped ship onto the other vessel, blowing a heartfelt, tender kiss to the Master and Commander who stood upright to attention and saluted her, respect and affection twinkling on his again-dimpled smile.

The captain of the merchant ship, robbed of his best hands on deck, had little choice but to detour to Bruges, which he did not want to do, as there was nothing there of interest or use to him, other than a handful of desperate men whom he could hire for a pittance. Orlando took this as her opportunity to land, and what was true of the captain was true of her too: Bruges held no attractions for her whatsoever and so—recalling faintly, as in a dream, an interest she once had, a fascination with, the city—she decided to aim for Paris: one of the nearest and also, though it belong to enemy land, one of the best.

Chapter 2 — In which Orlando makes the acquaintance of free-spirited women and men and realises she is, herself, quite the Revolutionary.

Many were the things Orlando was used to being able to do at his whim and fancy when he was a man, that she now, as a woman, found to be fraught with irksome complication. Travelling on her own from Bruges to Paris was one of them, and arriving in Paris during a revolution proved to be another. Some people may say that this would be obvious, but it was not obvious to Orlando, even though she had become aware of this new handicap to her constitution from the first day she had realised what, so as not to say who, she now was. With the constraints that decorum, dress, manner, speech, physical power and decency now put on her ability to manoeuvre, it mattered a great deal that she was a well to do member of the English aristocracy and had brought with her, securely sequestered upon her person, a not inconsiderable portion of her wealth, purely to cover for the eventuality that she might find herself in some need. And in need she now was: she soon recognised that the only way she would be allowed to journey in comparative safety and relative peace was to hire a coach and horses for her exclusive use and have it accompanied by not one but two British soldiers whom she bought free from a French garrison near Ghent, where they were being held captives as prisoners of war, a situation she knew about and was able to take advantage of—and this, it should be added, at a place she was able to reach—only thanks to the intervention of an elderly monk who saw it as his religious duty to deliver the damsel he perceived to be in distress safely into their hands under the borrowed cloak of one of his own order's vestments. It involved negotiations, parlays, transactions and parting with inordinate amounts of currency, but eventually the deal was concluded and Orlando could be escorted through a revolution-riven France right to the heart of the upheaval, and just in time for the second most momentous occasion in her prolonged progression towards a divestment of her king and queen.

If it was not without danger to traverse France in a southerly, or in fact any, direction as a woman, it was not entirely without challenge to establish a household in Paris towards the end of that summer, the year being 1789, and the government of the country having been wrested from the sovereign and given to the Third Estate, by the people making up that same 'estate', or certainly a significant proportion thereof, and therefore of the country as a whole, seeing that it, after the clergy and the nobility, made up all but two or three in a hundred Frenchmen and women. It was only just over two months since the Bastille, reviled emblem of arbitrary injustice and absolute power, had been identified as a source of gunpowder, stormed, occupied and dismantled, and Orlando soon found herself caught up in a heady mixture of political agitation and unending debates in the salons of the houses of the people she let know that she was in town and therefore was in turn almost immediately invited to. There was an intoxicating whiff of the new in the air, of ideas never heretofore considered possible, let alone plausible, of the equality of men being not merely an ideal to aspire to but an inalienable right, of the questioning of old rules thus becoming an inescapable necessity, of the deposing of the old regime therefore being the only reasonable course of action and, reason being the paragon of human achievement, of that course of action having turned imperative.

Orlando had had time, since her arrival in Bruges, to send word to Mr Pitt that due to circumstances so unforeseen as to adjudge them capricious, both on land and at sea, she had found herself unable to voyage to Russia and was instead now heading for Paris, an item of news that was greeted by the Prime Minister with dismay and relief in unequal measure. His relief, though undeniable, was moderate, but at least this meant that his agonised and somewhat long-winded, so as not to say incoherent, explanations to the Ambassador in Moscow as to what precisely the Lady Orlando might consider to be her business when she got there now proved irrelevant and superfluous, and that he no longer had to trouble himself with the prospect of answering any more questions about the purpose of this particular posting. His dismay, conversely, was large, because it also meant there was now something of a proverbial loose cannon abroad: an English member of society in Paris who was in constant danger of being kidnapped, murdered or, possibly worst of all, crudely indoctrinated with radical ideas. Then again, it was pointed out to him (and not, it should be noted, by his friend William) she was only a woman and would therefore pose no real threat to anyone, other than perhaps to herself, something which could be mitigated against by encouraging her to stay at one of her distant relatives' houses and to pass her time playing cards until this inconvenience of a revolution had blown over. That the inconvenience would be temporary, of this both Williams could no longer be entirely certain, but knowing that their own country had gone through a similar convulsion not so long ago and quickly seen sense, reinstated the king and since then practised a model of parliamentary constitutional monarchy with such success that the English felt entitled to call theirs the 'Cradle of Democracy', they were, though concerned, still relatively sanguine about the prospects of France similarly settling down presently into a new period of comparative calm: an optimism that all too soon was to prove, although well-founded, ill-honoured by the unruly French...

Orlando was surprised at how much and how quickly she felt at home in Paris. Like many an Englishman or Englishwoman, she had never seen cause to take either France or the French particularly seriously before, and the fact that they had grown into a powerful nation with an important capital city at its heart and a colonial presence abroad would have been an irrelevance to her, other than for the nuisance inherent in the French tilting the balance of power in favour of the rebellious American states and thus losing the British Empire half of the continent not long ago. But the spirited vigour with which both men and women, mostly of her age and across many layers of society now talked about the ideals of mankind and the nature of statehood, elevating the concepts of liberty, fraternity and equality to a rallying cry around a new flag that stood for the universal rights of citizens, irrespective of their birth, state or even creed, now filled Orlando's heart too with rousing passions and great hopes for a future quite different to any past she'd known. The French men and women whom Orlando associated with in turn saw in her a fresh and kindred spirit, a revolutionary in her own right, and they respected her for throwing caution so bravely to the wind and standing her own ground so resolutely. One or two, it was true, were not without suspicion: what of the two British officers she had freed and, their service of bringing her safely to Paris accomplished, released from duty so nonchalantly? Whence her articulate vocabulary in political affairs and the subtleties of diplomacy, as a woman? What of her scope of knowledge in history cultural, military and social? Only a spy, some surmised, could be so acquainted, only a spy and a *man* so equipped, quipped some others, but Orlando felt certain she had nothing to prove and set out to prove it all the same, more—as so often in her life was the case—by accident (or divine intervention) than by design.

Orlando had fallen asleep in the small hours on a *chaise* that was none too *longue* and far from comfortable, but several glasses of wine and cognac and many hours of avid conversation had made her head heavy, her heart weary and her legs seemingly non-existent, and so surrender to slumber she did. Her guests had continued debating for a while and then by and by had made their way either to their own homes in the vicinity or to one of several available guest chambers in the house Orlando had taken for the as yet indefinite duration of her stay. She herself, though, had been left to doze, as her small staff had long since gone to bed, and a parting guest had covered her with his cloak for a blanket. She had dreamt of Crete and of being held in the strong but tender arms of Hermes, and seemed, as in a distant memory, to recall the ancient treasures and the bold encounters of her travels, but she did so in a nonsensical, jumbled up, wild *melée* of scenes and characters and colours and voices that made for a frightful cacophony, when—minutes only after she'd shut her eyes as it seemed to her, though in reality some two or three hours had passed—she woke up to the beating of a drum and the riotous shouts and calls and clamours of a rabble. Orlando threw off the cloak, which she recognised as belonging to a young poet whose ebony locks and Roman nose made him appear not unlike a god in his very own right, she thought, and whose considerate gesture of leaving it here for her for the night gifted her with a wistful smile, heaved herself up to look out of the window onto the rue de Rivoli where—*lo and behold!*—a column of hundreds, nay thousands, of people was coming towards her and soon passing below. But they were unlike any crowd Orlando had ever seen: they were, almost all of them, women and they were not dressed like ladies, but wore the garb of fishermen's wives and market vendors; they were loud and brash, brandishing knives, banging on drums, and demanding bread. Orlando was riveted: she had seen scenes of riot before, in Constantinople; she had spent time with simple country folk in the mountains, but never before had she come face-to-face with the wrath of women scorned in their very existence. She threw on the poet's cloak, grabbed her convenient hat and ran out into the rain of this drabbest, but still most cataclysmic, of October mornings.

Orlando quickly caught up with the front of the march, and was able to make out the odd detail about its origin on the way: it had started in a corner of the market of the *faubourg* St Antoine, and quickly it had grown in numbers, in volume and in intensity, as first other market women and then other women and some men along the route had joined, and now, a couple of miles into the centre and past the Bastille, what had started out as a posse had grown into a battalion and they were going to get what they wanted: bread from the town hall, the *Hôtel de Ville,* just round the corner. Orlando couldn't help but march along, for of course they needed bread! Bread, she knew, had been scarce for the poor and risen in price to levels they could not afford, so how were they to feed their children; she herself, Orlando, would have given them bread from her own kitchen, had she thought of fetching some, but it would not have been enough for more than two or three dozen of them; better, surely, that they went to the stores of the city and took what they needed in order to survive.

At the *Hôtel,* near chaos ensued, as the women demanded not just bread, but weapons as well, and it was only thanks to the swift and diligent actions of a former guardsman whom the women knew and respected that they stopped short of burning down the building after ransacking its stores and held back from putting to death the store master too. Orlando was as intoxicated by the energy, the power, the hunger and the lust for living that drove these women, as she was scared of the fierceness of their cries and the anger in their eyes; but she was also inspired by their determination and convinced by their cause: *of course* it was wrong that the city held rich stores of bread for the wealthy few when the multitudes of the poor barely made it alive through the day. *Of course* the privileges of her own class here were too many, with none of them paying taxes but all of them living in luxury; and in fact Orlando was convinced that most of them knew this and wanted a change themselves, or if they didn't know it yet and were afraid of change, they could have it explained to them in ways that they would be able to understand. But right now, the change that these women proclaimed and demanded revealed itself to be one of a different and much more encompassing nature, and before Orlando knew it she was marching with the women of Paris out of the city and on to Versailles!

Chapter 3 — In which worlds collide and Orlando comes face-to-face with death, destruction, devotion, delight and determination (though not necessarily in that order).

It would not correspond to Truth sufficiently to stand up to close scrutiny if it were claimed by me, in this place, Dear Reader, that on her march from Paris to Versailles, in midst the shouts and calls and cries of the *poissardes* and their growing band of supporters—mostly women but also some men, and notable among them the aforementioned former guard and *vainqueur* of the Bastille, Stanislas-Marie Maillard—Orlando was not entirely in her element, even though, going on everything we know of her, nothing about her present circumstances at this time bore any resemblance to anything she had ever experienced before, and even though, among the noise of the drums and the rattling of the knives and the clanging of the makeshift weapons, she could barely make out more than every fifth or sixth word in any one sentence that the women, in their coarse and shrill voices, uttered to her, and even though not one of these women whom she had joined near the front of the march had so much as an ounce of understanding as to who Orlando was, or what compelled her to be there with them. But then neither did Orlando really comprehend what was happening to her, nor did she feel she needed to be able to decipher the words when the heartfelt tone of the voices she heard was so clear, nor did she have time to wonder at the surge of emotions that coursed through her veins, or how new and unprecedented they were: Orlando felt free. Orlando felt she was equal to them and they equal to her; not in wealth, not in standing, not in education, but in nature, in spirit and in power; and, yes, she felt she was among sisters. Six hours it took them to reach Versailles and at times it felt like a carnival, a parade, at other times it was dangerous and felt quite pointless. Rumours swept through the masses: the guards have been alerted, they will welcome us with muscats and cannons. The drizzle made their dresses heavy with damp and caked their shoes in mud; their feet grew blisters, their joints soon ached, but their righteous ire and their cause and their hunger drove them on, and Orlando did as they did and dragged her skirts through the mud and sang their songs, which she learnt as they walked; and as they walked, more people joined, and new rumours reached them that the National Guard had sided with them and was now on the march to Versailles to protect them; and other rumours still that their commander had warned the Royal Guard at the palace and all was already lost; but nothing to these women who had nothing to lose could be lost, and nothing therefore could stop them now, for they were on their way now and their demand now was not only that the king mend his ways and sign the declaration of rights, but that he come back with them and move his household to Paris, for in the rarefied palace and gardens of Versailles, which they had heard looked like an artist's impression of Paradise itself, he was not only out of reach but also out of touch and what king could claim that he ruled for the people if he was not in touch with his people?

When the women, and the men that accompanied them, arrived at Versailles, exhausted, wet, and—the supplies they had brought with them from the town hall having run out—even hungrier than before, they found that other women and men from the surrounding villages had received word and had come out to welcome them, and also here to welcome them were members of the newly named National Constituent Assembly, which was still at Versailles, having started out as the old *Estates-Général* earlier in the year. As the women piled into the Assembly chamber, proceedings in there became very informal, because over their shouts and demands, the speakers could barely be heard, and so while several of the politicians decided to mingle and converse with the women, none, it appeared, commanded their proper attention, let alone their respect; none, that is, except one.

Maximilien de Robespierre cut a fine figure with his handsome round face, friendly brown eyes and bright, approachable smile; wearing a dark coat of professional hem and a compact, unostentatious white wig that lent him a simple, dependable gravitas rather than frivolity or pompous decorum. He was a well-spoken man with an intelligent mind and, in his oratory as his demeanour, unambiguous and straight: he not only welcomed the women, he expressed their cause better than they had heard it expressed before. Not only did he have words of support, he had a grasp of their reality, so it seemed, and the women naturally warmed to him. If it was an age of reason, this, and if the movement that had been unleashed was one that embraced humanity and compassion and fidelity to the ideals of the common good, then no clearer, no stronger, no better voice could be heard to give it credence than that of Monsieur de Robespierre. But of all the women who had poured into the Assembly and were now lounging on the benches, nursing the blisters on their feet and drying off their hair, their hands and their faces, none was likely to be as rapt as Orlando, because, for all his rhetoric or their own democratic fervour, none saw in him an equal; what they saw in him was a sympathetic member of a different class, not the ruling class, for sure, but a separate class from them, for although he was, like them, a member of the Third Estate, he was, in every other way, unlike them.

Nor was he like Orlando. Orlando, as she understood herself to be, and as she had no cause to understand herself otherwise, was a lady of considerable wealth and social standing, and although almost nothing about her current appearance betrayed any of this, she was nevertheless, by dint of this, her 'birth', part of the nobility (depending on how far back we allow ourselves to look into her unusual parentage, partly possibly also of deity, though neither she, nor anybody else, seemed, at this particular moment, likely to be at all aware of this). Significantly, also, Orlando, unlike almost any of the women around her, was educated, and educated not only in the basics of literacy and numeracy, but in a classical, even philosophical sense, which is why it was now with unabashed fascination and a great deal of comprehension that she was listening to this young politician, by profession, as it turned out, a lawyer, who talked a language she had never heard before: one of real, profound radicalism. Each man should have a vote, he declared, none should live in fear of death as a form of punishment, the National Assembly, of course, must be the seat of power in government. The women did not expect more of him: none argued they, too, should have the vote, and few thought it at this point. The demands he made not on their behalf only, but on *everybody's* behalf, were sound and reasonable, and as he spoke, the anger, the fury, the danger abated: the women knew it in their hearts, they would get their way; and when the king agreed to receive a delegation of them, they went, a half dozen of them selected from their midst (Orlando not among them), and returned in no small measure charmed and pacified and furnished with reassurances of food; and when, somewhat later in the day, came forward the promise of the king's impending signature on the Declaration of the Rights of Men and Citizens, some felt that this battle was now surely won. Indeed, a few, surrounding the former guardsman Maillard, had already begun their long journey home, although most kept milling around the grounds awaiting the final outcome of events.

After he had spoken, Maximilien de Robespierre was wandering about the Assembly, chatting here and there and listening intently to what the *poissardes,* in their, to Orlando, incomprehensible patois had to say, apparently untroubled by their choice of words or their pronunciation, either of which had, during the day, sufficed on numerous occasions to make Orlando's hair stand ever so slightly on end. As she sat on a bench that resembled a giant, rectangular, leather-upholstered *pouf,* watching him make his way through the throng, never once putting a foot wrong, never once wavering in his attention, never once yawning or demurring or betraying any sign that any of these women were anything other than ladies who had every right to be here and postulate their grievances and voice their demands, Orlando felt a flame of emotion kindle within her that she had not felt in a long time. Not since, as a slightly younger man, she had espied across the ice of a deep frozen river the exquisite shape of an even younger Russian princess had the part of her belly just below her diaphragm so felt alive, had her pulse so inexplicably quickened, had her breath so readily grown rapid as now; now, she knew long before she could reason, she felt long before she could speak it, she feared long before she feared she might ever regret it, she fell in love and her love was so powerful, so compulsive, and yet so serene, that she couldn't but sit there and watch and wait and know that within minutes he would pass by her and he would see her and he would—gentleman that he was—recognise in her what she saw in him, and would look into her eyes, the deep brown pools of his pupils as large and profound as hers, and he would smile his irresistible smile and extend his hand and bow ever so slightly, and she would rise and curtsey in a manner completely commensurate with his bow, and this would be the end of the matter and also the beginning, for what else would there now remain but for him to lead her by the hand, without words, without poetry or protestations, and guide her to his dwelling near the rear of the palace, where, humble though it may be, it would still be palatial to them and afford them, over several hours and long into the night, a heavenly, sun-god-sent paradise all of their own. And that is precisely how matters now did unfold.

When on a previous and outwardly similar occasion we found it advisable to draw a veil of discretion over the proceedings and let human nature take its follied course, we now find ourselves compelled to accompany the dashing lawyer to his apartment, together with Orlando, for there were many matters that engaged their minds much more and long before they gave way to other, no less passionate, but for our eyes less seemly urges. For naturally these two were attracted to each other, how could they not be; and naturally they beheld each other favourably—this stands to reason when both were favoured with such favourable aspects—naturally, too, they delighted in each other's company, when the thrill of recognising their emotional equal in the other rippled through each of their nerves and sinews, but beyond all that they quickly uncovered, in a few minutes of conversation that led them from the Assembly hall to the private chambers of the Assembly members, that theirs was a meeting, also, and maybe foremost, of *minds!* And what minds these were: agile, curious, nourished yet hungry for more, open to the movements and accidental actions of people on earth as much as to the motions and prescribed paths of the stars in the skies. Nothing was so sacred as not to be questioned, nothing stood so high as not to be reached for, no scope was so wide as not to be encompassed, within the mind itself. Maximilien de Robespierre might have found this kind of connection with another man as easily as with a woman, he felt – more easily even, perhaps, because there was in the coming together of minds something noble, and pure, they both felt: in the abstraction of thought from the messy business of intercourse on the physical plane there was, to them both, exultation. And now, naturally, their talk was of Rousseau and Montesquieu, and of course they discussed, and delighted in, Voltaire, and beyond that in Descartes, and Locke and even Immanuel Kant.

You will forgive me, Cherished Reader, if at this point I once more shy away from relating in full all aspects appertaining to the story I have undertaken to acquaint you with, and do not venture to delve into the particulars of their discourse, as their discourse was variform and expansive on subjects ranging far, ideas reaching wide, questions probing deep and ideals scaling high. Such was the nature of their discourse, and the intent, and the substance, that the hours passed in compressed concentrates of themselves, and before either of them was able to feel the fatigue that was bound to creep up on them after such expenditure of thought and breath, the sun again began to make its wondrous presence felt, not yet by rising above the parkland trees and shining its glinted rays upon the water fountains in the gardens, but as an aura before dawn: the purple-hued glow that ascends slowly as it chases away the darkness of night. Orlando should have slumped and sunk into her Louis Quatorze chair from weary tiredness, considering that she'd had little sleep the night before, conversing, as she did, at length with her friends at her own *salon*, and bearing in mind, furthermore, that she had walked, at not a moment's notice or preparation, thirteen miles in the rain alongside rabble-rousing women whose chants and shouts and curt-phrased talk she could not understand; and yet Orlando was wide awake and fully alert to the speeches of this man, for although Orlando was his only audience, he addressed her with the energy and conviction of an orator, and conversely when it was her turn to speak, Robespierre sat rapt in silence relishing each finely formulated phrase in the well-taught French that Orlando so faultlessly produced. Sometimes, as when it came to the barbarity of state-sanctioned executions, torture and coercion, they agreed; often, as when the extension of universal suffrage to both men and women was discussed, they clashed; sometimes, as when the existence of an all-knowing, all-powerful, all-benign but in his or her ways most mysterious Divine Being was examined, they knew not how to say with precision what they meant but respected that they meant different things in different ways and, temporarily awed by the imponderability of the magnitude of their deliberation, fell into a moment of agreeable silence, during which the ongoing din and never-ceasing hubbub, all through the night, of the women camped outside—who had since been joined by, and were bantering with, the National Guard—was the only thing that penetrated their peace; and then a brilliant quote or a magnificent insight once heard or read or invented in another debate or right now off the cuff would come to either of them, and, like a spark jumping from the amber into the tinder, a new blaze would crackle with heat and light and the all-consuming yet life-rendering force of intellectual fire.

It was towards the sixth hour of the morning of the sixth day of October of the year of the Lord 1789 that the noise of the clamour outside the palace grew louder and the clanging of footsteps inside grew faster and the general hum of a large mass of people being about swell into a regular commotion, and as Orlando and Robespierre went to see what was the cause, so early, when the light of the day was only just beginning to filter in through the majestic glass windows, of such unrest, they saw that some of the crowd had entered the palace through a side door and were looking for none other than the queen herself. Panic and fear quickly gripped the few members of the Royal Guard dotted about the palace and within minutes a shot rang through the marble court, and another soon followed, and cries went up, *murder! execution!,* and a lifeless body was carried outside, which elicited screams of pain, loss and anger among those who had come here, and more and more of them, now more hurt, more enraged, and more savage than ever before, stormed into the palace, seeking out guards, finding them, beating them, pulling at their uniforms and hair, tearing into their flesh and breaking their bones and sawing off the head of one of their number, small as it had been to start with, and sticking it on a pike and parading it outside to the cheers and the jeers of the masses, and another guard fell and the queen ran from her chambers across the palace to bang on the king's chambers' doors, where by a hair's breadth she and her maids found refuge, and only after further long minutes did finally the fury slowly abate, and some semblance of calm was for the moment restored as the members of the National Guard who had come in support of the marchers cleared the palace and entered a dialogue with their brethren from the Royal Guard; and seeing this horror and rage and uncontrolled rampage, Maximilien de Robespierre bethought himself of the danger that was here for a member of the English aristocracy and offered, nay insisted, to usher Orlando out of the reach of the women she so boldly had marched with in solidarity.

Orlando was not afraid for her safety but she was appalled at the scenes of violence she witnessed and she was glad, at this moment, to be helped into a carriage and to be sitting next to the man she had spent an entire night with in a pure exchange of ideas, and within minutes of pulling out of the gates, as the road ahead of them lay open and straight and the horses' hooves fell into a steady canter, she could no longer resist the drooping weight of her eyelids and, tilting in unconscious comfort against her protector, she finally, finally fell asleep.

Chapter 4 — In which Orlando wakes up in a near-stranger's arms and resolves to stay within his embrace for just a little while longer.

Orlando could not tell how long she'd slept, nor could she hazard a guess what hour it was; she could not make out, through her sleep-worn gaze, what house she had been sheltered in, nor did she remember for several long moments which city this was, what country even, or what century. All had, for her, blurred into one: she could not say if what she felt was real and what she now remembered was a dream or whether this was still a dream and what she had experienced was real. The look on the face of a man she would only later learn was named Tardivet, staring down at her, severed, cruelly and crudely, from its shoulders and triumphantly but without ceremony stuck upon a pike, had haunted her sleep and she was sure now, as her body began to compose itself into waking, that she must have tossed in her sleep, and turned, and maybe cried out; she had been afraid, after all; the bravery of her previous day now shook her to the core and she shuddered so hard that the arm and the chest against which she had been resting her head now moved a little and, with a groan, the man the limb and the torso belonged to also came to and from a dishevelled round face those clever, kind eyes looked at Orlando, and the man's lips formed into a charming grin that made Orlando give off a girlish laugh. Like naughty children they laughed, and Orlando now remembered it all, and in sequence, and she knew who this man was who had spent the night sitting up next to her, allowing himself to be used as a prop, as a cushion, who had somehow evidently succeeded in heaving her up from the carriage—she remembered the carriage, and the horses bolting through the gates of a palace invaded by a bloodthirsty mob—into his apartment here in the centre of Paris, and who had made no attempt at soliciting, given no signal to want, invited no demonstration of feeling, anything other than an amicable, and entirely mutual, affection, of the kind of respect and, yes, the word here seems appropriate, devotion, a gentleman would afford a good friend. When Orlando had, from the first, been drawn towards this man who in physical height was not even her equal, but who in stature succeeded in making himself appear solid and large, she now, at last, felt the urge to surrender, and surrender, without further ado now, she did. All of a sudden, now, the words were none more: their eyes gazed into each other and with their bodies already so closely aligned, that thing that exists between two human beings when everything that needs to be said has already been said, and everything that has not yet been spoken can be said without words, now took over and not Orlando nor her host knew who now led whom as they made from the *chaise* of the *salon* to the *lit* of the *boudoir,* dispensing with pieces of clothing one at a time while moving along.

Now, then, is the time to draw that veil of discretion we earlier felt we could do without, for nothing so ill pleases the Diligent Reader as to have his imagination sullied by depictions in public of what belongs in the private sphere. Suffice it to say that once again it was not a sphere that Orlando felt willing or bound to leave in a hurry. What Monsieur de Robespierre lacked in bulk and build he made up in prowess and skill and Orlando for one had, her more recent acquaintances notwithstanding, not before experienced quite the like.

Orlando might have stayed with Maximilien de Robespierre for a goodly while longer: she did not easily tire of an intelligent man's society at the worst of times, and these, by any standard, to her, were verily among the best of times, and they were so for Monsieur de Robespierre too. In fact, history was to show, not so long after, that while Orlando had yet in store for her many encounters and experiences that could match this and any previous ones—the arc of her existence reaching so uncommonly wide across the fabric of time—de Robespierre really would never in his comparatively short life delight in anything quite so resoundingly joyous and blissful as these few days with Orlando. Yes, his fame would rise, and his significance in the world had far from peaked, but where the fountain of happiness was concerned, he did well to drink from it in gulps of unrestrained pleasure now, because for him it would soon dry up, not ever to replenish again. Neither of them could know this, as they lay in each other's arms, in the promising young man's bed, having partaken of each other without guilt or shame or regret; and in the relative quiet of a momentarily peaceful Paris morning, their thoughts did turn to the future and to tasks in hand, and maybe this is what poets have meant when they have spoken of a Paradise Lost, because now they suddenly found, having tasted of the tree of knowledge of each other, that they were no longer as at ease with each other in matters of the mind as they had been before. Perhaps the gloss of a beckoning fruit obliterates and outshines any blemishes that, the apple once eaten into and its core now perching exposed on the sideboard, conspire to make it look rotten, or if not rotten then at the very least spotted with flaws. Questions that had previously seemed matters merely of opinion now in the light of a newly drawn dawn revealed themselves to be fundamental, and where Orlando and de Robespierre diverged, the chasm that opened up between them was no longer easily bridged. Foremost on Orlando's mind, having more, and more wide-ranging experience of living, both as a man and as a woman, was how could from a revolution so radical and encompassing as this the entire female sex be excluded and, as seemed to be the intention of her lover, banished away from the platform of politics into the domestic domain of raising and nurturing offspring? More categorical, still, and even more difficult to reconcile for Orlando was the pull of the instincts, of 'nature', to one type of behaviour, when the push of the intellect, of 'civilisation', so clearly dictated another. Orlando felt not at all inured to this kind of dilemma and it disturbed her to find that no matter how great, how capable, how inventive a mind was at work, the most basic forces were never entirely tamed, but rather, they seemed held at bay, but how securely and for how long, no-one could tell.

"Yet, is it not always thus?" enquired of her Robespierre. He knew, as did she, that the moment was approaching when they would have to part, but it troubled him to see her so troubled, and he sought to cheer her and revive her spirit and in reviving her spirt fan a little her passion for him, not for it to be consumed once again, but for him to know that they parted as friends, and not only as friends, but as veritable *conspirators* who could believe in the ideals he believed in and who would find ways always to hold them up high. "Why should we," he further argued, "measure ourselves by our failings, suffer ourselves to be judged by our faults? All men have faults, have they not, and so do all women. Is it not then the cause that we embrace and the purity of our intention that may lead us to glory? Not glory for ourselves but glory for the people in whose name we have thus embraced the cause? Allow that we should be imperfect, Orlando: expect not to be beyond reproach. Demand of yourself that your design be noble, thus will the road that you take lead you ultimately to your goal."

Orlando was not convinced she would find it so, but she smiled at him, and seeing her face returned to good weather, he smiled her his bright and knowing grin too and they kissed, and Orlando got up from the bed and she spake: "It is time that I should leave you to proceed with your revolution. Remember me in your hour of need." She did not know whence the thought that he might soon face an hour of need had entered her mind, but entered it had and so she gave it expression, and washed and dressed and made to leave. Maximilien de Robespierre, having watched her, jumped off his bed and dashed around her, and fell on his knee before her just by the door and said: "Lady Orlando, will you marry me?" Orlando looked at him with kindness and, making sure not to laugh, but with friendship and warmth in her voice, said: "That, I fear, Monsieur de Robespierre, would be going one step too far." And, ruffling the short tuft of hair that was forever normally hidden under his wig, but now lay innocent before her like that of a child, she left by the staircase that led to the door.

Chapter 5 — In which Orlando reflects on her mission, reports back to the Williams and as a reward for her labours is promised a posting to Prussia...

Orlando remained in Paris for nine months precisely. There was no symbolic meaning nor was there any natural imperative for this particular period being allowed to elapse before she once more undertook a strenuous journey; it was, as is often the case, merely a confluence of coincidences that appeared to conspire to make it just so. During all this time, she had no more conference with Maximilien de Robespierre, although their paths on a number of occasions crossed nearly and once also really and on that occasion they both seemed delighted to recognise and acknowledge each other, but nothing more. For Orlando to recognise de Robespierre had become exceptionally easy because in the months after their encounter, he rose to the top of the revolutionary pile and was seen in person and depicted in print frequently; that he in turn should so immediately remember Orlando could only be less obviously attributed to the impact the time they had spent together had made on him and of course to some not insignificant extent also to her strikingly handsome appearance.

On the anniversary of the storming of the Bastille, the 4th July 1799, Orlando was out in the streets with her friends, old and new, with the students, the women, the poets, the philosophers, the Americans and the English as well as the French, and, as one of them put it, they danced with their arms locked together and their hearts open wide; and their voices rejoiced as all was still hopeful and good. Paris, capital of the erstwhile most powerful nation in Europe, had changed that nation's destiny forever, and the drivers of this change had been the people: not the already powerful, not the elite, the First or the Second Estate, but the common people, the Third Estate, the people of the workshops, of the boutiques and of the professions, the people of the markets, even, the women, the *poissardes,* who had come to fetch the king from his palace, and who had actually succeeded in doing just that: the royal family had come back with them from Versailles to an empty, abandoned Tuileries palace in Paris, where the king, resigned to his fate, had asked to be brought a copy of the History of Charles I of England: he whom the English had executed during their revolution only four decades ago.

It was in no small measure that revolution which elevated the English among the celebrants now to the status of cherished guests, for their French brothers and sisters saw them as kin, their forerunners, their pioneers who had achieved what they now too were going to achieve, to turn their absolute monarchy into a parliamentary monarchy, in which the king would be a servant to the people and not the people serfs to the king: it was a goal worth achieving, and achieved it now practically was; and nobody, on that heady summer day only a year into their sea change, could know or foresee what was about to befall them. Even those who had never liked or trusted the king, nor let alone his coquettish Austrian queen, did not predict that he would attempt to flee rather than commit himself to the new order, and none who knew Robespierre could have foretold that his name would soon become forever synonymous with The Terror, that this man who had spoken so eloquently against capital punishment would soon preside over the execution of the king and the queen and thousands upon thousands of others who were to be deemed, or even just suspected of being, enemies of the revolution. None, perhaps, other than Orlando: Orlando, by now, and possibly so equipped through the many and varied and often unorthodox experiences she had been permitted to gather since first she set off, as a simple shepherd youth, from her island in Crete, nearly two thousand years ago, possessed a sixth sense for these matters, and it was this unquantifiable sense, this disquiet, that prompted her, shortly after the anniversary celebrations, to arrange for a passage home before the tide in

Paris would turn again, and the mood change from hope and elation to suspicion and paranoia instead.

William Pitt and William Wilberforce were surprised, each of them, how delighted they both were to hear that the Lady Orlando was safely returned and desired to dine with them once again so as to better acquaint them with her observations—she was going to use the word 'adventures', but then thought better of it and tore up the note and started writing it over again—in France. It had been as she had stood on the deck of yet another ship, sailing past the white cliffs of Dover, that she had found the time and the peace and the quiet, at last, to reflect upon her time in Paris and the things she had seen and partaken of there, and she imagined herself, as if in a dream, sailing towards Alexandria once again, and this reminded her of the purpose and the reason she had set out in the first place, and she realised that she hadn't paid any attention to, nor made any investigation into, not even sought any further knowledge of, the fabric of the city of Paris. It was as if it had passed her by, it had held no meaning for her, no importance: yet it was a fine city with an exceptional cathedral and boulevards that would be the envy of any ambitious mayor, or, for that matter, slightly vain god; but she hadn't, she now had to admit to herself, given them any thought. What she did bring back from this city was neither learning, an education and wisdom, as she had done from Alexandria, nor was it art and architecture and science and maps, as she had done from Florence, nor was it characters and their stories, as she had done from London; what she was carrying with her newly now was a sense of self as a woman and as a human being and an ideal of what a society could be, but also a deep understanding that the differences between human beings were small, that the greats who described human nature and fought for the rights of men and spelled these rights out in charters and who spoke in the loftiest terms of the values of mankind, were all, when it came to it, just as human and as susceptible to the same simple foibles and desires as everyone else, and that chief among these desires was, after all, perhaps simply the desire to be desired in return. And this, while gliding toward Albion, had made Orlando smile to herself, for she knew a thing or two about desiring and being desired...

The dinner at Downing Street, to which Orlando so routinely had invited herself, was held in the embrace of an atmosphere that was markedly different to the one she had encountered before she had left for, ostensibly, Moscow. When, at the time, the two Williams appeared to be indulging Orlando for reasons that they themselves could scarcely explain, and the conversation was, on their part, always, if polite, then also somewhat bemused, because neither of them could, if truth continue to, as it has been, be told, really be entirely certain why Orlando was even there or who, precisely, she genuinely was, then now, by contrast, they seemed to know exactly why she was there, and who she was, and they hung upon her every word, taking it in and asking innumerable questions about Paris, about the French people, about the king, about the queen, about Robespierre, about everything, and Orlando became aware, as she was relating what she had seen and experienced, that the Prime Minister was exceptionally nervous about the developments in France and that his disposition towards the revolution was rapidly evolving and becoming more sceptical, critical and apprehensive. Orlando in turn felt some unease, because when at previous dinners she had been full of exuberant enthusiasm for her taking on an ambassadorial role in Moscow, she now wondered whether what had turned into an extended stay in Paris was forcing her, retroactively, into the role of a spy. Orlando was anguished about this thought, because she by now counted many of the people she had met and associated with in Paris her friends and she could not be at ease with the notion that anything about what she was saying could be construed or let alone used against them in an involuntary betrayal.

The Williams both seemed to understand, and they reassured her, and thanked her, profusely, and suggested there may be another post for her, in the foreseeable future, in Prussia. It would not be the first time, nor would it be the last, that Orlando ended up not quite where she was supposed to go, but for now that did not matter one jot to Orlando; Orlando was glad to have been of use somehow, though how exactly, she couldn't tell: still, she felt she had been of use to the intellectuals of Paris, she had been of use to the *poissardes,* she had been of use to the man who was turning into the leader of the French Revolution and she was being of use to her Prime Minister, and therefore, by extension to the country and to the world, and that, for Orlando, was, though not everything a woman could wish for, good enough to be getting on with just for the time-being...

IV

Manner

Vienna

1905

I have, since my arrival, settled into a routine that is both pleasurable and conducive to stimulating my mind, which is as much as to say that it is doubly pleasurable.

When the sun reaches through the tall, south-east-facing windows, half ajar, to tickle my cheek on the pillows of the gigantic bed I call mine own, I slowly wake to find myself in a large, spacious bedroom that defies the word 'chamber,' through every aspect of the generosity with which it is appointed; its straight lines, its elegant edges, the mirrors and the solid but light-coloured woods, the unselfconscious sparseness: nothing clutters or burdens the morning, and as I rise and go about my ablutions I feel that the unfolding day is truly mine. (More than one of the guests at my infrequent and very modest receptions—miniature salons, one might say—for the artists and writers of whom there are many in this town, have told me that the building, the furniture, the fittings and in midst of all these, I myself, reflect a *Zeitgeist* that is truly 'modern,' although I, myself, am not entirely certain what exactly that means.)

I dress, in keeping with my surroundings, simply, and the simplicity of my style is such that it by necessity gives me the appearance of a man rather than that of a woman. It is not the case that I wish to negate the beauty or distort the delicacy of my sex, yet have I had to realise that while my sex has long awoken from the slumber of ignorance and indifference which it had mostly been lulled, partly perhaps also allowed itself to be lured, into, and has begun at last to assert itself in science, art and, somewhat tentatively, still, in politics, neither in science, art nor politics are the majority of men as yet prepared to even acquiesce to, let alone fully accept and respect, us women as their peers. My tailor has, however, on account of my slightly taller than average height and slenderer than common build, found it easy to make me a range of dark trousered suits, shirts, waistcoats and coats that allow me at all times to appear in public practically yet respectably attired; and ever since I have found this to be so, I have, to my not inconsiderable delight, found also that while I attract frequent glances that linger somewhat too long and betray a moderate level of bewilderment, and in some cases wonder (in some, more rare, cases also hostility), I get approached far less often than used to be the case by gentlemen of a certain age and signally more often by very young people of an artistic inclination, and for very different reasons. Naturally, as in everything, there are some notable exceptions, one such I shall speak of anon.

Further in keeping with my mode of clothing, I have my hair cut short and comb it close to my skull in just a hint of a wave that, given its natural disposition to curl, is unavoidable, but has the advantage, perhaps, of easing somewhat the stern line with which it otherwise would frame my face. I have, for some considerable time now, given up the habit of using a walking stick (ever since I gave my favourite one away to a dashing sailor in London, as it happens) and of that I am today particularly glad, for Vienna is a lively, busy place where oftentimes an ability to manoeuvre quickly can make the difference between reaching the *Café Central* in the *Herrengasse,* just behind the theatre, intact, or being run over by an electric tram. Their inherent and curiously imposing, for unwavering, danger notwithstanding, I like these stout little urban trains with their funny, insistent bells, urging horses and pedestrians out of their way, even though I rarely have reason to use one myself, as everything I need can be found within easy walking distance of my flat and the new, broad *Ringstrasse* to which not long ago the city wall has given way and which now encircles, as its German name suggests, the beating heart of this burgeoning town. My rooms are on the fourth (which is the second highest) floor of the building the architect Otto Wagner had built to form the corner of the lefthand *Wienzeile* and *Köstlergasse,* and so while my ceilings are not quite as high and stately as they are on the second and third floors, my outlook is splendid and the sun reaches me soon after dawn. There is an electric lift in the centre of the staircase that leads down to the street, but I so enjoy sweeping down the comfortably spaced steps that I rarely if ever use it, especially not on the way out: I walk, nay run, down the stairs, holding on to the banister and relishing the airy dry clacking sound that my feet make on the bare stone flooring as I seem to glide toward ground.

During the agreeable late-summer months, it is invariably early that I leave the house, and as I step out on the pavement, I feel at leisure to inhale the city that gets on its way to work: clerks and civil servants heading for their offices, shopkeepers making their way to open their stores, bankers and brokers; traders and cabs. The artists and poets have not yet woken up, by and large: mostly they will surface later. I walk up the *Wienzeile* towards the opera, and this is in fact a little detour: a shorter, more direct route would take me towards the museums, but that would cut out the most extraordinary building I as yet know of in Vienna, and possibly also my favourite, the *Secession*. The locals call it 'the golden cabbage', on account of its gold-leafed dome, and many are none too fond of it, but every time I walk past it, it brings a smile to my face as it proclaims, in German capital letters affixed to its bulky exterior "*DER ZEIT IHRE KUNST, DER KUNST IHRE FREIHEIT*"—to each age its art, to art its freedom—and my heart feels a little lighter for this, straight. In the summer, I reach the almost forbidding, fortress-like walls of the *Secession* too early to go in, but now, as the autumn leaves are gathering about the tree trunks dotted around it, the rising sun rouses me later in the morning and so by the time I get here I just find it open and often step inside to look at the art.

It is a dreamy, wondrous but also unsettling world my new good friend Gustav and the artists he has gathered around him exhibit here, full of unspoken desires and gold-plated, irregular patterns that seem to evoke both a gilded glamour and a deep anxiety beneath it, not at all like any art I had ever seen before; and his women are not only feminine, radiant and gracious, but also haunted and daunting and possessed, in equal measure, of tenderness, challenge and a deep melancholy. No wonder the old guard of the Vienna establishment were appalled by his works, but credit is due to the city and its authorities for giving him and these new voices in art a site here right in the centre to make themselves heard.

Not too long ago, I went around Gustav's to pay him a visit, as on occasion I do, and as I walked into his studio there was a slender shadow of a figure silhouetted dark but brittle against the brilliant whites, in varying shades, of a dress so effervescent it seemed to rustle, even though the air was as still as the woman wearing it in the painting. She looked different from the other women I had seen painted by Gustav: yes, she was confident, yes she looked strong, and yet her skin and her eyes had the vulnerable sheen, still, of a girl; but this one, more than any other, looked hopeful, with her half-open half-smile, and her pitch hair tied in an unruly bun. I slowly moved closer, as one who fears she might disturb an encounter of profound communion, and indeed more than with any woman I had ever seen brought to life by Gustav, this one seemed to be ready to turn around any moment. I was almost afeared she might do so and admonish me, just with a glance, not harshly, for interrupting her session, but there was no woman sitting here for the artist, there was a painting, finished, as far as I could tell, albeit with hardly any colour in it, and certainly no gold at all, and there was this poised presence of a man, a boy really, cap held with both hands, as in devotion, his lips half parted, just like the woman in the picture, but his not in a smile; his dark eyes fixed on her shoulders, bare. And he did turn around to me:

'My sister, Margaret.'

Still he didn't smile, but rather directed his attention back to the woman he claimed as his kin, now a puzzled expression cast over his face.

'And who are you?' I tried to sound gentle lest I might scare him.

'I am Ludwig, her brother.'

'I see.'

I did not see, nor did I understand, but the youth seemed to think that that was all I needed to know, for the moment, and if nothing else that it eminently, logically, followed. Then he added, as if fleetingly recalled:

'Mr Klimt is not here yet.'

'Not to worry.'

'Will you have coffee with me?'

'By all means, Ludwig.' I felt a sense of relief at this innocent, pragmatic suggestion: 'Let's go and have coffee, together.' At this last word he gave me a quizzical glance, of the kind a teacher might give you when you have said something that is either quite silly or stating the blatantly obvious.

On our way to the *Central*—he insisted we go to my 'usual haunt: do not, under any circumstances, alter the structure of your day because of me,' even though I offered him a slice of the really rather exquisite though undeniably rich chocolate cake they serve at the *Hotel Sacher,* or to have ourselves quaintly served by the old-fashioned waitresses of the *Demel Café,* the *Demelerinnen,* at the *Michaelerplatz*—Ludwig told me that his brother, Rudi, had now taken his own life too and that he often felt that that was the only right thing to do, but that he himself was clearly too young for it, still. And now did it dawn on me whom I was walking with through the city: Gustav had mentioned a short while ago that his chief benefactor, and the man who had financed the building of the *Secession,* had lost a second son now under most tragic, most unwarranted, indeed dreadful circumstances. Gustav was too upset to narrate it in detail, but his patron was a powerful and widely known man and Gustav clearly cared a great deal for this family.

'My father will not have Rudi's name spoken in our house. And do you know why?'

I knew, now, who this boy was, but I didn't know why his father was so aggrieved as well as bereaved by the second self-inflicted death of a son of his that he would so compound his pain as to disown this son.

'He loved men. Physically, you know: he longed for them, at least as much as for women, probably more. That's why he killed himself. Imagine this: he was so alone, he felt so ashamed. Over a thing like that. I know it is forbidden, but so is suicide.'

He told me how his father had commissioned Gustav to paint a portrait of Margaret for her wedding. A faint memory fleeted through my distracted mind of a portrait I once sat for, for a lady...

'Your father is Karl von Wittgenstein,' I finally declared, having reached the conclusion moments before, 'how old are you?'

'I shall be seventeen soon. You haven't told me your name.'

'Orlando.'

'You dress like a man and you call yourself by the name of a man. I salute your extraordinary freedom.'

With that he doffed his cap and proceeded to light himself a cigarette, whilst continuing our walk, but not offering me one, perhaps thinking—not unreasonably, for a boy of his generation—that it would be uncouth for a lady to smoke in the street, even if she was dressed like a man, or maybe, and this immediately seemed more likely, he was just too preoccupied by his own turmoil to think of the niceties of politeness:

'I also am lost, you know,' he said, his pace unexpectedly

energetic as he strode across the *Opernring*, dodging, like everyone else, the tram, 'in just the same way that my brother was, and in other ways too.'

Then he fell into silence, and as his brows seemed to knot themselves in concentration not to do with the traffic of carts and people and bicycles and horses but something altogether more confounding, I allowed this silence to be and steered us toward the grand *Café Central*, where I found, to my relief, my preferred table unoccupied, and my favourite waiter on shift.

'*Den Fiaker zum Frühstück ohne den Obers, und für den* Herrn?' I was almost certain Leopold, our waiter, a tall perpendicular man approaching his sixties, gave me a wink as he stressed 'gentleman' ever so slightly when asking what he might be having while reciting my usual. Whether that was because the 'gentleman' was so young, or because, unlike me, he could actually claim to be one, I didn't know, but Ludwig demanded a strong black coffee and sighed:

'I am condemned to dwell among idiots.'

I was about to reprimand him, albeit mildly, for disparaging the old man who, after all, had never been anything other than courteous, even charming, to me, but Ludwig was not referring to the waiter, his mind was elsewhere:

'My so-called peers, the pupils at my school in Linz, do you know what they chant after me when I tell them I shall be spending a day in Vienna?'

I had no way of knowing and no reason to guess.

'Wittgenstein wandelt wehmütig widriger Winde wegen wienwärts.'

I thought that was quite clever and had to suppress a chuckle. Instead I attempted, somewhat clumsily, I concede, to make him see the funny side too:

'And do you?'

'What?'

'Stroll wistfully towards Vienna owing to contrary weather conditions?' I tried to coax from him a smile. Ludwig did not smile. He fixed me with his unwavering stare and said:

'I take the train, there are two in the morning and two in the afternoon, and I come to Vienna because I need some semblance of culture, I need to escape, at least once in a while, from the morass of mediocrity they have me stuck in.'

I tried to think back to when I was sixteen, it felt so, so long ago. Did I have a sense of irony then? Maybe not...

'What *is* language, Lady Orlando? What is it, that can *actually* be said?'

Ludwig looked at least twice his not just proverbially but also literally tender years now as he swept his thin arm across the room and declared:

'None of these people, none of them, actually know what they're saying. At any time. Their words are *without exception* meaningless.'

I felt sobered, almost humbled, as he continued:

'This is what I have to deal with, *every day of my life.*'

I could not instantly and obviously see why Ludwig, son

of possibly the richest man in the Austria-Hungarian Empire, felt that this, of all things, was what he had to deal with every day of his life, when most youths his age would contend themselves simply with dealing with their first amorous crushes (be they on boys or on girls), and cramming for their exams.

'*Nobody* is capable of thought. Real, abstract, clear, clean, uncluttered thought. Yes there are one or two people who think unusual things, I take it you have read Otto Weininger, going by the way you dress, but he is not right about anything really, nor is he that original, nor is he abstract; he is obviously deluded, but then so was Jesus, then so am I.'

I did not want to get into a discussion, at this time of day (it had only just gone eleven) about Otto Weininger, another young man who had taken his own life only about a year or two ago, and whose views on women and Jews I would have thought laughable, were they not quite so earnestly argued and therefore quite so disturbingly potent, and had they not clearly the power to impress themselves even on an intelligent mind, such as Ludwig's. Ludwig must have sensed my alarm, for he moved the conversation on swiftly:

'I am reading Schopenhauer, but I am not at all sure I am that impressed with him.'

I had to ponder this for a moment, because I, by contrast, had not properly studied Schopenhauer and rather skimmed him as far as I could remember, but then something different occurred to me:

'Frege thinks.'

'Frege?'

'Gottlob Frege, yes. If you read his *Concept Document on a Formula-Language for Pure Thought,* you will find, I believe, him to be quite abstract, maybe sufficiently so.'

Ludwig's face lit up, for the first time all morning.

'I shall read him. May I see you again?'

'Of course you may. You will find me here, about this hour, every day of the week.'

'Thank you, Lady Orlando.' With this, he drank up his coffee in one sharp swig and left, with a spring in his step.

A gentleman of middling years, sitting at a table or two removed, turned his head as he watched him leave and, turning back around again, caught my eye, for I too, was watching Ludwig leave, a little mesmerised by his intensity. The gentleman did not smile but made as to clear his throat and rose, picking up from the table a notebook and a pen, and from his neighbouring chair a pair of gloves and a scarf, which, for reasons I couldn't discern, he had not left with his coat on the coat rack by the entrance. Slowly—more slowly than I thought his healthy age would render necessary—he walked across the café that was by now beginning to fill up with its lunchtime clientele: mostly young men from the offices nearby who had no wives yet to cook their main meal for them, and who clearly had neither ability nor intention to do so themselves. He looked dignified and paternal, with a fast greying beard and warm, kindly eyes; he was immaculately dressed and had a slightly bent-forward gait of the kind that you find in a man who is used to walking with his gaze fixed on the ground, not lost in thought so much as searching his mind.

'Dr Freud,' he introduced himself, without hesitation, yet with a curious formality that seemed to suggest he imagined his name might ring a bell and one none too pleasant at that, but his name rang no bell with me: I did not remember having heard it before.

'Would you allow me to sit with you for four minutes only.'

The precision in his request made it impossible to refuse, and in any case I was not going anywhere, for like many of the early luncheon time patrons now settling down at the tables around me, I was in the habit of having the chef's special of the day, whatever it happened to be: it made for another simple and therefore agreeable aspect to my routine and there was plenty of variety in the dishes throughout the week, whilst the afternoon's activity provided ample opportunity for merry improvisation.

'Please,' I replied and offered him a seat almost next to me, but he chose instead to sit opposite me, with his back to the rest of the room, perhaps, again, I thought, because he felt he might be more than necessary conspicuous otherwise.

'I could not help,' he began, with the tone of a man who weighed his words carefully, as one who knows that whatever he says will be listened to and whatever the listener receives may be acted upon, or, if not acted upon, then internalised and felt keenly, 'overhear some, by no means all, in fact I am glad to reassure you only odd snippets, of your conversation with the young man who looks to me strangely familiar.'

'He is quite remarkable, in his own, it might be suggested, somewhat precocious manner. It is possible you may know his father.'

'Quite so. In your conversation I furthermore could not help—I hope for this you will forgive me—catch your name.'

'Lady Orlando.'

'Indeed, which, in turn, sounded familiar, I had heard it mentioned, once or twice, in social circles as well as by patients of mine, always uttered in admiration and sometimes wonder, and I have often been intrigued: how is it, if you will forgive me what must seem unpardonable impertinence, that you dress in the way that you do; is there a reason that you consciously know of?'

Now a little bell of recognition faintly did begin to chime: it was the word 'conscious' that made me recall a volume I had been given by a young woman who regularly attended my very humble gatherings and she had pressed a book into my hands, saying 'you must read this, Lady Orlando, it is sensational, revelatory. Dr Freud is delving deep into the unconscious mind...'

The book, entitled *Die Traumdeutung,* dealing in detail with the interpretation of Dr Freud's own and his patients' dreams still sat near my bedside table, mostly unread, but I now felt I could place my interlocutor and I also had an inkling now why he may have thought that recognising his name would not with absolute certainty be bound to elicit only generous feelings in me, as amongst Vienna society he was considered quite controversial. About this, however, he need not have worried.

'I am, Dr Freud,' I told him in my most measured voice, intending to set his mind at ease, 'aware only of that which I can be certain I know, and what I can be certain I know in this regard is that sitting here on my own with my *Fiaker* for breakfast, with or without the whipped cream,'—I could have sworn I perceived the edge of Dr Freud's upper lip quiver with just the slightest of whimpers at the word 'whipped'—'that strolling about town in the afternoon as I shall be glad to be doing soon after lunch, not least as it aids my digestion; that returning here later in the afternoon for maybe a *Mazagran,* and then attending a dinner and a concert or a performance at the opera, in or outwith the company of a friend'—this time Dr Freud's lower lip curled slightly upwards as if in contemplation of the meaning of the word 'friend' in the context of my person—'would be well nigh impossible if, at first glance, the world here in Vienna perceived me to be what I am: a woman.' At this, Dr Freud nodded gravely. 'Perceived, on the other hand and by contrast, at least at first glance, as a man, I immediately change the framework of that perception, and although most people very quickly recognise my sex, I have, by means of costume alone, demolished the barrier of their resistance. Granted, for most I am now an exotic bird of paradise, who can and must be regarded with both suspicion and admiration, but I am, strange as it may seem, no longer a bird of prey, seen to be out to devour, who must therefore, in turn, be devoured first.'

Dr Freud at this ceased to nod, put his ungloved hand upon mine on the table, looked me straight in the eyes and enquired:

'Lady Orlando, will you come to my practice and speak to me more: of your dreams, of your desires, of your childhood, of your unspoken secrets, of your perspective on the experience of your sex: you are ahead of your time, I believe, and I am writing an essay on human sexuality—surely the deepest, most mysterious, but also most powerful force that drives us—and a free spirit, such as yours, may be able to yield profound, untold insights; I promise you, by everything that I as a doctor hold dear, I shall never reveal your identity.'

At this point Leopold came around with a small piece of paper that served to describe the chef's special of the day, and with eyebrows raised full of high recommendation, he announced this to be goulash and *Semmelknödel,* and so, as one can't eat dumplings alone without seeming either obstreperous or forlorn (or possibly both), I invited Dr Freud to lunch with me, rather than giving him an answer just yet.

Dr Freud, with perfect manners, accepted the invitation and forthwith desisted from asking any more questions that could, in one way or another, be construed as related to his work, or answers to which might, in an off-guard moment such as one is prone to encounter over a bottle of *Grüner*

Veltliner, turn out to say more about one's self than one might otherwise have wished to divulge. Instead, Dr Freud steered the conversation to those particulars of my life whose substance may be considered to amount to 'small talk,' and chief among these, he was keen to learn what had brought me to Vienna.

'I was,' I confided in him, 'all set for a posting to Prussia, specifically to Berlin; but when I got there, I didn't feel convinced that Berlin was quite ready for me.' I did not mean to sound enigmatic, but I had received that general impression when I had alighted there from my train and sensed, inexplicably, that while the city would soon have its moment, that moment had not yet properly come, and so I boarded the next train taking me further east, venturing that perhaps—and here I realised I veered perilously close to broaching a subject of professional interest to Dr Freud—something subconscious in me was still drawn toward the East where so long and so often I had longed to be, yet never quite managed to go.

Dr Freud was most sympathetic: 'Ah, the East: it exercises a pull on the sensitive soul...' and I thought for a moment he was going to make a note in his notebook, but he refrained and instead moved both notebook and pen out of the way, as our *Vorspeisen* arrived on the table. In the comfortable silence that followed (of the kind that allows the lingering thoughts to bed down to rest and make way for new, more alert ones) I experienced that strange but widely familiar sensation of having been here before, of having had this precise exchange with this very gentleman in this location some time ago, a fleeting moment of experiencing the present as a memory. I described this to Dr Freud, who nodded, once again gravely, and said: 'as if you'd already seen it.' I indeed felt I had seen this before, even though very clearly I hadn't, but Dr Freud was interested in something else I had said, which he referenced to Berlin:

'Do you often have premonitions?' I assumed from his posing the question that he wasn't working on premonitions as a psychological phenomenon and readily affirmed: 'I do. Not premonitions, perhaps, so much as a strong sense that things are going to go one way or another.'

'Where do you think things will go in Vienna?'

'I am not sure, Dr Freud. You have a great deal of liberty here, today, a wonderful panoply of creative invention: someone like me is allowed to be as I am, provided of course I am not what I am, and there is a liberal feeling of not only embracing, but positively planting, prodding, generating, the new. Perhaps it has to do with the turn of the century: maybe the old century having been so momentous and so fast, and there being in the air an atmosphere of the pace moving forward accelerating still further, there is a need now to have a *caesura,* to have done with the old and worship the new.'

At my use of the word 'worship,' Dr Freud again frowned:

'What altar, may I enquire, do you worship at, if at all?'

'I know there are those who worship at the altar of science, and there are those who worship at the altar of art; I can't claim to be doing either, Dr Freud, nor do I have a religion, as such, I am searching—isn't everyone—but not, I believe, for meaning so much as for patterns.'

'How most fascinating,' Dr Freud agreed, and, almost as an afterthought, offered: 'why no religion?'

I wondered, for a brief moment, whether allowing the topic of our conversation to slide so readily into religion from which it would, invariably, have to descend into politics, was appropriate in the given context, but reminded myself that this was not a dinner reception or some diplomat's *soirée,* but an impromptu luncheon in a Vienna café, and so I explained:

'I have, though bold a claim this may sound, a perhaps uncommonly wide perspective on religion, drawn from my own experiences and observations in different parts of the world and I feel, without wishing to overstate the matter, somewhat related to civilisations which had no need for, or at any rate no understanding of, the concept of an all-powerful deity, and so having seen, over the last few centuries, the great religions that have emerged from the Middle East—Christianity, Judaism, Islam —fight so fiercely over territory both literal and spiritual not only against each other but also amongst themselves, fills me, I hope you will forgive me for stating this so bluntly, with a categorical sense of unease: have we not science, humanity, compassion and the intellect to understand each other as human beings and resolve our disputes and divergent priorities in a civilised manner? For certain, I have not known a single age, in all the time I have an awareness of, that has not in one way or another been riven by conflict and war, but should we not have evolved past this, a long time ago? I feel that if I were to subscribe to a particular religion, in the way that religion is today understood, I would have to negate so many others, and neither would seem to me in the least bit sensible, humble or, therefore, right.'

As I looked at Dr Freud, having so made my statement, I realised, with a small jolt of excitement and awe, that I had never spoken like this to anyone before, that I had just formulated, in one simple paragraph, my stance on something as fundamental as religion, purely at the prompt of a pertinent question. No wonder, I thought to myself, Dr Freud is turned expert at probing deep into people's minds: he listens better than anyone I had ever met.

'Yes. I like to put it thus,' Dr Freud now said quietly, in a tone that no longer was that of a doctor so much as that of a troubled father: 'the voice of the intellect is a soft one.'

'So it, is Dr Freud, so it is! But that only means that it must not rest until it has found a hearing!' I was quite excited about this; I sensed the descent into politics happen swifter than I'd expected, though fully expect it I did, and now I really did no longer mind:

'You must find the tenor of your mayor disquieting?'

'I do. Mr Lueger is a popular man, he both is the voice of the people and he has the ear of the people. So when his rhetoric incites hatred and condemnation of Jews then there is more than a small possibility that his seeds of suspicion will fall on fertile ground: there are many malcontent people in this city and many are only too eager to lap up the words of a demagogue, and among those many, there are, though it grieves me to say so, many who are very young.'

The pall of a shadow settled over Dr Freud's pensive features, as he slowly continued: 'We are, you see, once again an easy target, Lady Orlando: there are many of us here, and many of us do well. If you are in a sizeable minority you are a noticeable outsider, and if as a group you are seen to be doing well, you naturally attract attention, and not just in the vein of pure admiration, but also of envy and scorn...'

'The problem is they control everything, getting rich in the process: parasites!' a young man chipped in uninvitedly, spitting out his generic insult aimed plainly at Dr Freud. I hadn't noticed him at all, he was one of the people who had taken their seats at the tables around us over the last half hour or so, and he did not stand out from the rest in any way; he appeared, to all intents and purposes, completely normal. I didn't know what startled me more, the casual, matter-of-fact manner of his aggression or the paranoid hatred that it so failed to contain.

I looked at Dr Freud with alarm, but he demurred: he did not think it worthwhile, or fruitful, to engage in an argument with a stranger over lunch, nor did the stranger seem to expect being so engaged, he turned around again and demonstratively, noisily opened his newspaper over his plate. In the silence that followed, embarrassment and anger both welled up inside me, but Dr Freud continued calmly eating his goulash and when he next looked up and still found me staring at him, his lips eased into a smile, and quietly but audibly, so it could easily be heard not only by me but also by our discourteous table neighbour, he said:

'There will always be those who project their own insecurities, inadequacies and genuine traumas, be they lodged deep inside from their childhood, or keenly felt as current frustrations, onto others. It doesn't matter whether it is us Jews, or somebody else: by diminishing the other, the self feels comforted, reassured, valued. If I, or you on my behalf now, respond to this erosion of our dignity in kind, we get sucked into a cycle of reduction, diminishing each other to the point of elimination. And that is why there is no point entering into an argument right now, it only makes matters worse by confirming an already deep-seated prejudice. I see this played out in relationships all the time.' I was unsure whether I agreed with Dr Freud that a pronouncement such as the one we'd just been subjected to should ever go unchallenged; did not, I wondered, the fact alone that it remained unchallenged serve to make it appear 'normal' and 'acceptable', even 'right', when clearly it was none of these, but I too was not in the mood for a confrontation and it certainly was not my intention to expose Dr Freud to further embarrassment by causing a scene in a café where he, I surmised, was no less a regular than I (though we had never met before: it is, after all, a large, bustling place) and so we both continued our meal, a little subdued, perhaps, but soon finding topics of conversation of considerably greater cheer.

*

I was glad, after such an intriguing morning in the company of young Ludwig and so thought-provoking a luncheon with Dr Freud, to spend a little time composing myself during a walk in the charming surroundings of the *Volksgarten,* before making my way across the lavishly spacious *Rathausplatz* towards the *Berggasse* for my appointment with Dr Freud, which I had finally, over coffee, agreed to, at three o'clock, after a patient he had already booked in before me. I did not know what to expect and I certainly did not consider myself a 'patient' in that sense, but I decided to offer myself to Dr Freud's new practice with an open mind, while he in turn reassured me he was not proposing to conduct or initiate a course of 'psycho-analysis' with me (which would take months, if not years), but that he simply wished to hear me talk with a view to gaining some insights for his ongoing research.

And talk I did. Relaxing on a couch with a propped up headstead, heavily draped in an oriental patterned throw with large, soft velvet cushions to sink into, I eased my mind into a state of almost drifting, holding on just enough to be aware, to my right hand side, of the seated figure of Dr Freud, facing away from me, listening. It felt to me like the first time anyone had ever actually listened to me at all. As I spoke, recounting my life, my dreams and my memories—those that stood out among their near-infinite multitude—reaching as far back as the island of Crete, my wondrous encounter with gentle though mischievous Hermes, my first voyage at sea, the marvellous teachings of Euclid in Alexandria, my wonder at the aesthetic perfection in the works of Michelangelo and da Vinci in Florence, the heart, the soul and the mettle of the Queen of England and the encompassing spirit of her people in London, the righteous, fiery ire of the women in Paris and the democratic passion of Robespierre, through to the deep searching souls into meaning and self here in Vienna, I felt that I had lived for, literally, ages, and yet my thirst for knowledge, my awe at beauty, my love of humankind, my yearning for freedom and my curiosity into existence had not been nearly exhausted.

As I was talking, in a quiet, unhurried voice, there formed in my mind the images of the people, the scenes, the cities, at first almost reluctantly, beating off frequent interruptions from very recent memories and trivial worries or little thoughts of no substance, but gradually all these distractions and interferences gave way to a steady, low-keyed stream of consciousness on which neither I nor anything within me found it necessary any longer to impose a structure or meaning or purpose, other than to let it flow and in doing so perhaps allow some pattern or connection to reveal itself. When the hour concluded, I felt light and unburdened and I thanked Dr Freud for his time, but I did not book another appointment with him nor enquire about his fees or what conclusions, if any, he drew from what I had told him. Instead, I said:

'I think you may be on to something invaluable, Dr Freud. It feels as if you'd allowed me to access my unconscious mind and I don't know how it appears to you, but to me it appears as the part of the iceberg that lies under the surface of the water, with the conscious mind making up but its tip at the most.'

Dr Freud smiled at this analogy and said, somewhat cryptically:

'I never claim to understand my patients, Lady Orlando, but I feel I comprehend you instinctively, fully; how odd that we should have encountered each other at this particular juncture, and yet also how apt: perhaps everything is just as it should be, after all...'

I made my way back by almost the same route as I had come, through the *Rathausplatz* towards the *Central,* but not without making a small detour to the *Votivkirche;* I am not greatly enamoured of its neo-gothic style, but it is surrounded by a lovely little park where I now sat for a while in the afternoon sun, right next to the university building, thinking about Dr Freud. With my eyes closed and my head slightly upward inclined to feel the warm rays on my cheeks, I noticed, after a short while of such exquisite peace, a shadow cast itself over my face, depriving me momentarily of the sun. I opened my eyes and it took me a moment to make out, against its brilliant light, standing directly in front of me, an earnest young man with a scruffy leather bag and a portfolio folder under his arm. I shielded my eyes and squinted at him and he took this as his cue to address me:

'Would you perhaps like to buy some art from Vienna?'

It struck me as a curiously phrased question, but considering how well, overall, the day had been going so far, I felt it would be nothing short of churlish to not at least appraise the art on offer.

'Why don't you sit down and show me what you have?'

He followed my invitation to sit down next to me on the bench, in the slightly awkward manner that very young men often have when they are still getting used to the extent their limbs have grown to; and in the tone of someone who is not yet fully in command of the modulations of his voice, he apologised, more sheepishly than I found the situation required, even belatedly, for troubling me so. I told him he was no trouble to me at all and encouraged him to open his portfolio, which he did with a studious care and just enough of a juvenile's clumsiness to elicit from me a near-motherly smile. (This I say with some level of speculation since I have not, of course, ever yet been a mother nor do I think it likely that I shall be one soon, nor, therefore, ever.)

The watercolours he showed me were nice. Friendly street scenes in Vienna, a courtyard here, a parkland there: a little gauche perhaps, but then he was very young. I asked him how young and he answered, in an echo of something I'd heard once before that same day: 'soon seventeen.' Did he want to become an artist, I asked him, and he said 'yes, I would like that.' And then, with a tint of sadness in his eyes that has haunted me since: 'very much.' I liked this young man, he was, I felt, in oh so many ways so similar to young Ludwig whom

I had met in the morning: earnest, a little world-weary in the way that boys of his age nowadays seem to be (when I was a boy of sixteen, I had no time for world-weariness: I needed to sit under a tree and enjoy the view of the sea and dream of things that might never be, although, as I soon was to learn, of course, there is no such thing as a thing that can never be...), but courteous and sincere. As I leafed through his portfolio he watched me intently, and it occurred to me that, his very young age notwithstanding, he really needed the money he could earn from selling these pictures.

'I get by,' he said, in reply to my question whether this was his sole source of income and whether there was no-one looking after him, and I left it at that, because I did not want to hurt his pride. Was he new to Vienna, I asked, he said yes, he had recently arrived, after finishing his secondary school in Steyr where he'd gone to after a stint in Linz, which he didn't like.

'Linz? You went to school in Linz, did you?

'Yes, my father wanted me to go there, I didn't like it.'

'You weren't by any chance friends with Ludwig von Wittgenstein, were you?'

'I knew who he was, his family is well known; they are very wealthy, everybody knew who he was, but he was two years ahead of me, we didn't really speak to each other.'

I was going to ask, 'you're exactly the same age, how come you were two years behind?' but thought better of it, as this, I surmised, might be a sore point. Instead I traced my way back to one of his paintings, a small, delicate one in which the fastidiousness of some of his drawings and other watercolours had given way to a freer hand in which the colours were allowed to bleed into each other and create their own natural patterns; I was struck by the fact that hardly any of his paintings depicted people, and if so they were small, slightly bent figures or almost unnoticeable shadows in the landscape. This one was a landscape with nobody in it, and it needed nobody in it either, it was a gentle work of art that came from the inexperienced but dextrous hand of, I was certain, a fragile young soul who wanted, like everybody else in the world, nothing so much as to be respected and allowed to flourish and thus, if I allow myself to put it so simply, to be loved.

'You have not signed your work, my friend,' I said to him, and this jolted him into action, almost as if I'd scolded him, and he took a black coal pencil from his brown leather bag and put the letters *A. H.* in a curiously spidery hand to the bottom right corner of the painting. I never asked him how much he expected for his art but I gave him a couple of notes I had on me and they seemed to more than suffice, for his eyes lit up and his face creaked into a beaming smile, which made me think that maybe nobody had ever bought a painting of his, or none without haggling over the price, or perhaps nobody had ever asked him who he was, and so I said to him:

'You should send your work to the Academy of Fine Arts, you do have a talent,...' I glanced down at the open leather bag on his knees which had written inside its folding lid his full name, '...young Adolf.' At this he looked at me with large brown eyes, like those of a startled rabbit, and so, as much to soothe his fear as to coax his curiosity, I continued: 'If you haven't been before, go to the *Secession* and ask to speak to Mr Klimt there. Tell him Lady Orlando sent you. Have a look at his work and that of the others exhibiting there: they are finding entire new ways of showing us the world and us in it. It's exciting: you might find inspiration there.' He seemed more than a little unsure, so I added: 'Some of it takes a bit of getting used to, but that's what art is about, is it not? Bringing out our inner selves in ways that surprise, delight, and also challenge us?'

He folded his portfolio and stood up:

'You have been very kind to me, thank you,' he said, and bowed a little bow, almost like the one I once received from a sailor, some ten or eleven years older than he, and turned to leave.

'He won't bite you, you know!' I called after him, and of all the things I have ever said to anyone, I wonder about this one sentence the most: was it wise, was it appropriate, was it necessary? I meant it not only as a joke, but also as a genuine encouragement, but when he turned around to me, and now with the descending sun directly on his gaunt, unloved face, I saw the fear again in his eyes: no hatred yet, no elation, no anger, no joy: only fear, and for this fear, I in turn feared he may not take up my advice and invitation, and my heart went out to him, for at that point, and with his modest ambition to nurture his talent and become an artist, I did wish him well...

*

My day was finally allowed to return to its ordinary pattern, as I found myself back at the *Central* for my long longed-for rum *Mazagran,* and because it had been an unusually colourful day, I permitted myself two in a row. I was reflecting on the people I'd met and on what I was doing here in Vienna. (It wasn't that unusual for people to approach me: because of the way I dressed I stood out, and because I stood out some people, especially artists, musicians, poets, or someone investigating human nature, like Dr Freud, felt they had licence to speak to me, but the day had lodged itself in my mind for its density.) And I thought to myself, I shall stay here for a little while yet, for who knows what the future may bring, good or ill, but there are too many interesting things happening here to leave this city just yet. Besides, I had no urgent reason to go anywhere. My supposed 'posting to Prussia' had been all but a smokescreen and I could not yet foresee an imminent time when I, as a woman, would be allowed to take on the role of a diplomat, or a businesswoman conducting my own enterprise. Even as an artist I would not be taken seriously yet, I suspected, nor as a musician. Perhaps as a violinist? I had no talent for the violin, nor any taste for it either. I could, quite conceivably, make a name for myself as a writer: Orlando has a sufficiently male ring to it and almost any surname I chose, from whichever estate might suit me, would certainly do.

This 'being a woman' now vexed me. Rarely had it vexed me before, as I had largely been able to coast through the day with my pleasant routine, seeming benign and content and above all *interested* in everything and everyone, but now it suddenly irked me to think that in the phrase 'I am a woman' there was contained, in the minds, in the view, of still a vast majority of the people around me—both women and men!—that insidious adjective 'only'. I was expected, after all, was I not, to think not 'I am a woman,' but to think 'I am *only* a woman,' possibly with a mock-explanatory, 'after all' as its tail. I don't know was it my hour with Dr Freud that prompted, now, all of a sudden, my anger; I had so very rarely in my life been angry before, and considering the life that I'd led I felt I had very little if any reason to feel angry at all, but now it welled up in me and I was certain at once that this just won't do. There would be the need for a fight to be fought, and soon. It was not a case of an inconvenience any more, or of a god-given place into which, immovably, my gender was cast; it was a case, surely, of man's will, of centuries, nay, millennia of culture having shaped it thus; and culture, I knew too well from experience and had again seen so radically, so categorically and so swiftly in Vienna right now, could change and could change completely in no time at all.

At last I felt in tune with myself once again, and I resolved to go home and get changed and attend tonight's dinner—a fairly ordinary affair at an ambassador's residence, given in honour of some promising composer called Schoenberg—dressed in a full-flowing gown, complete with enticing jewellery and very uncomfortable shoes. Now, while the impact I have on people around me when I dress as a man is, for reasons that will be obvious, considerable, my appearance as a lady is—and I say this not in vanity or as an aggrandising self-compliment, but merely as a statement of easily observable fact—simply stunning. Gentlemen respond to it in a way that is wholly predictable, but, for all that, no less flattering, whereas the ladies' response tends to be no less predicable than the gentlemen's, though flattery rarely comes into it. Nevertheless, feeling liberated by wearing my costume of femininity as a matter of my own choice, I commanded the room, and much as the gentlemen's praise and appreciation, so the ladies' reaction adhered to every rule in the book: from pained compliments given through gritted teeth, to swift turning heads and ill-whispered salaciousnesses intended not for the confidant's ears as much as for mine, to even one or two heartfelt, genuine exclamations of admiration and congratulation, the dames of Vienna society that evening ran the gamut and I, I daresay, took it all in my stride, for tonight, after all, I was not 'only a woman,' I was *Lady Orlando,* and I cared naught.

'There will come a time,' I found myself impressing upon a stoutly bearded fellow, leaning onto his shoulder for fear of losing my balance in these murderous shoes whilst holding on to my *sekt* glass with a hand that was drawing circles far too wide in gesticulation not to spill some drop here and there on the protrusion of his substantive rump, 'when a woman may not be a queen just by birth, but a *president!* Such as they have them in *America!* Elected by her people, on account of her *worth!*'

The gentleman whose name and calling in life had already escaped me though they had deeply impressed me only moments earlier, gave me a sideways glance not altogether unperturbed, but instead of arguing with me or laughing at me he merely said, 'oh, *absolutely!*' and gave me a smile so sweet I simply had to kiss him right there on the lips. I was, of course, very drunk, and it is to Herrn Schnitzler's unending credit that he resolved not to take advantage of me, but called for my carriage and saw to it that I was safely brought home.

I dreamt my most vivid dreams that night, no doubt fuelled by the many fascinating conversations I'd had during the day and the many glasses of sweet Austrian sparkling wine I'd drunk during the evening. I shall not go as far as to recount my dreams, as I am acutely aware that one's dreams are never nearly as interesting to anyone else as to oneself, but I was disturbed to find, when I woke up long before the sun had any chance to tickle my face, and not at my usual leisure at all, but with a vehement jolt, that my dreams had been in turns violent, erotic, sensual and confused, and all of the above at the same time: Gustav's stark portraits, the young street artist's diaphanous drawing, the music played by the promising composer, which seemed to have neither a beginning, nor a middle, nor an end, and yet still appeared to evoke something profound at its core, the Viennese in Mr Schnitzler's play... – that's what it was! That's what caused the unrest, I was certain: he had told me about a play he had written; it had never been published yet, nor even performed in public, but the idea was so simple, so provocative, so true: just couplings, across the spectrum of Vienna society, the whore with the soldier, the soldier with the maid, the maid with the young gentleman, the young gentleman with the young wife, like a merry-go-round, on and on, until the cycle comes back to the whore, and I wondered, now lying awake in my bed, on my own, why is it suddenly so much on everybody's mind? Is it that we have all collectively woken up to what's there, or have we somehow put it there and are consequently now forced to deal with it?

I was sure, glancing out at the waning moon, that sex used to be incredibly simple by comparison. Everybody engaged in some kind of sexual activity all the time but nobody ever really spoke about it, at least not since I'd left Alexandria. They may have alluded to it, punned on it, made clandestine reference to it, but it had been, for centuries, the thing that everybody did but nobody mentioned. And now, suddenly, everybody seemed to talk about it, express it; in words, in art, in dance, even in music. And I thought of Ludwig's poor brother, and young Ludwig too: it felt like another eviction from Eden, a second loss of paradise. Nobody, when I was a sixteen-year-old in Crete, would have dreamt of taking his life on account of just his desires. And I remembered the conversation I'd had with Dr Freud about religion and it dawned on me, only now, just how confining a prison religion had been and still was. No wonder so many were now at last trying to break out or at least create for themselves some space to move within. I felt I began to understand what Nietzsche may have meant when he started to claim that 'God is dead.' And I remembered a curious question Dr Freud had asked me: 'Do you often have premonitions?' It didn't seem strange to me then, but reflecting upon it now, it puzzled me greatly, and it puzzled me even more how readily, how naturally I had replied to him, 'yes I do.' What is it, I wonder, that gives us a sense of foreboding, an uneasy feeling that things are about to change, that they are about to go ghastly, awry. Is it maybe simply that we pick up the signals, register them, internally process them without even noticing that that's what we are doing, all the time? Is it maybe nothing more and nothing less than our subconscious mind beginning to understand the connexions that exist between things and events and circumstances and is trying to alert us, urging us to change course?

I did not have a sense of foreboding at this particular time, but I did feel that there were very conflicting forces at work, all around me. And were I a painter, a composer, a writer, or anyone at all of significance, I thought I should find it necessary to start to take sides, to state who I am, and to show what I stood for. And maybe that is true of everybody in Vienna—perhaps it is true of everybody in Europe!—today.

After lying awake for what seemed like a couple of hours but may in fact only have been twenty minutes, I dozed off again, this time in a deep, sound sleep, from which I awoke, in the manner to which I had become so agreeably accustomed, with the first warm stroke of the sun across my humming head. I began the day much as I had begun the previous day, and as I begin every day here in Vienna, and on this day I was fortunate in that Gustav was at the *Secession* as I popped in there, overseeing the hanging of a new exhibition. I told him of my encounter with a young budding artist and he said, 'of course, send him along, I shall be happy to show him around and look at his art!' I was somewhat relieved to hear that, even though I knew that Gustav was a kind and open man who habitually showed a great interest in the work of young people. He in turn told me he'd had word from the young Wittgenstein that he was in town but was unable at this moment to come and see him, because he was too busy reading a book by Frege. He himself, Gustav, had never read it or even heard of it, but from what he could tell, Ludwig was riveted, which was always a good thing, Gustav felt, as nothing is more exciting for the curious mind than a challenge. I would have loved to have asked Gustav to come to the *Central* with me, but I could see he was busy and I was certain that I should not tempt him with any distractions right now, so I took my leave and ambled there by myself, drawing in the autumn air that was already filled with the morbidly pleasant spice of decay.

When I got to the *Central* I was surprised but in no small measure delighted to find none other than Ludwig sitting at 'my' table, and his entire demeanour had changed. He was alert and energised, fired up:

'Thank you,' he said, before I'd even had time to offer a greeting, let alone sit myself down: 'This,' he patted a book that evidently belonged to a library, 'is *exactly* what I've been looking for.'

'I am so glad,' I said, nodding at Leopold who simply mouthed at me from a distance to make sure I wanted the usual, 'you have already read it?'

'Of course not. I have looked at it, all day yesterday and all night last night. I have hardly slept at all. I don't understand a single thing of what he is saying, yet, but I will. Mathematics: there is purity in it and the purity is logic, and in logic I can breathe...'

I didn't know what to make of any of that, but I thought it was probably well. Still, I needed some topic of conversation and so I enquired, a touch lamely:

'What will you be doing after school, do you think?'

'I don't know, Lady Orlando, there are too many choices, but I shall go, I suspect, to Berlin, we have a family friend there at the *Technische Hochschule*. I shall find something to study, I am, as you know, an unwritten book.'

And here, I confess, my heart grew weak and it melted. I cannot quite describe the feeling, nor can I find a fit and proper reason for it, nor do I wish to absolve myself from any guilt or responsibility, only, perhaps, in as much as I had long since abandoned the need for guilt whilst always accepted the imperative of my responsibility, and so I stand by what happened next. Something within me gave way; it may have been the extraordinary confluence of experiences, insights and emotions of the previous twenty-four hours, it may simply have been the new, fresh light in his eyes, it may have been the actual genuine warmth of the moment; whatever it was, I deliberately, purposely, did something that I hadn't done in a long time: I set about to seduce him. I felt, deep inside, that this boy was aching to become a man and that if there was one thing I could offer him at this instant, it was no further long conversations, no greater ideas, no clearer abstraction from life, but a full day's worth of living. 'Would you,' I said, and already I noticed the change of tone in my voice—it happens so easily, so readily, so gladly, when the timing is right—'like me to show you my library at home? It has nothing in it that may be of obvious interest to you, but it offers a great deal of privacy...' I thought there was no point in beating about the proverbial bush with him now.

I couldn't tell whether Ludwig got my meaning or not, and nor did I particularly care: I shall take him to my apartment, I thought, and things shall unfold in the way that they please. This time, Leopold's look, as I settled our bill with him, was one of mildly appalled admiration, as he seemed to comprehend the meaning of our uncharacteristically swift departure completely. But Leopold was of a generation of waiters who had by now really seen and heard it all, and I had no worry that from his lips would ever escape any gossip or scandal.

I did not wish to subject Ludwig to the prolonged awkwardness of a walk lasting some twenty minutes, and so I hired a hackney carriage just outside the *Burgtheater.* Nor did I want to waste time, when we got home, pretending that there was anything about my apartment or my library worth contemplating other than us ourselves, and so once we were sitting next to each other, with Vienna drifting past us at the clonkety pace of a middle-aged mare, I held, in my soft-leather gloved hand, the hand of Ludwig and squeezed it down ever so slightly onto his thigh: he didn't look at me, but I think he did wince, just a little...

We were lying next to each other, the sun still reaching through the room's south facing window, just, enjoying that peaceful glow of fulfilment, that content, when he turned his head to me and, in a natural, instinctive gesture that would seem studied if it had to be learnt, ran his thin long fingers over my neck and my collarbone and then looked up and into my eyes and said, 'you are very beautiful.' I smiled at him, because I knew it was true. Many people have described me as 'beautiful' and many have meant it, but at that moment I believed it was actually so. The anxieties and the niggling irritants that find their way through the cracks of an imperfect life no matter how unencumbered an existence one leads, they all seemed at bay, for an hour or so, as we lay there, in more or less silence. I couldn't help, looking down at the shock of mousy hair as he nuzzled his head into the comforting cavity he had just described with his hand, thinking of the boy whose watercolour was lying next door on a table. What made them so different, what, so much the same? Ludwig here was not confident, he wasn't in any sense 'strong', other than in his intellect and his will to pursue that only which was of interest to him and to him made some sense. I didn't even think he was particularly happy, in fact the opposite: like many a searching soul he was quite morose and full of self-doubt. But—and as this thought formulated in my mind I sighed a bit and as I did so, Ludwig noticed and raised his head with an inquisitive look until I patted him and kissed his hair and he lowered it again, once more at ease—Ludwig, unlike the young artist, had no fear in his eyes. He had anguish and insecurity and he was torn by his love for his best friend Pepi at school, as he'd told me; he had sadness and the loss of his two elder brothers, he knew loneliness and isolation and he felt, as he also had told me, sometimes, in fact often, like an alien from another world, but he had no fear. Maybe he needed to have no fear, because his large family was always there for him still, because his father, though strict, respected and loved him, because his razor sharp mind would find him a way? I don't know. But being without fear meant he would be able to live his life without hate.

A few weeks later I bumped into Dr Freud and I wanted to ask him a thousand questions that had, since that memorable day, clustered around my brain. He asked me, 'how are you, Lady Orlando?' and I wanted to say to him, 'Dr Freud, I am really exceptionally well, thank you, but there are so many things I now need to know.' Instead, however, aware of the burdens he already carried on his shoulders and knowing that in the end I would have to, like everyone, go and find my own answers my very own way, I just said: 'most excellent, Dr Freud, thank you, and you yourself?' To which he replied, with a glint in his eye: 'most excellent, Lady Orlando.'

Today, as I go about my routine in old Vienna, a city that to me seems a City of Dreams, I feel strangely serene. I shan't stay here much longer, I feel it will soon be time for me to move on. But the memories I have made here will linger, and mostly, in the most enjoyable way.

Before we said goodbye, Ludwig and I, on that afternoon—it was getting towards sundown and I felt ready, soon, for my *Mazagran*—I caught him standing by the window, now fully dressed, but his shirt still loose hanging out of his trousers. He looked very much like a schoolboy right now and I wondered had I made a horrendous mistake. He had furrowed his brow and seemed stuck in a thought, rather than merely lost in one, and so I asked him: 'Are you feeling all right, Ludwig? Is there something troubling you?'

'Yes...' he said, without turning his head, which left me momentarily worried, '...I mean no.' And that didn't clarify anything. I thought it would be best to allow him to unstick his thought by himself and proceeded to sit down in front of my large frameless dressing mirror and tie my own tie. After a little while he came over and stood next to me and we looked at ourselves, there, making a very odd couple indeed, but a handsome one too, and one, I knew, that would likely be never together again. His face was still tense with a question, and so, looking at him through the mirror, I asked, once again: 'What's on your mind, Ludwig?'

'There are things,' he said slowly, as if he was coaxing the sentence from his own contemplation bit by bit, 'of which we just cannot speak.'

I thought for a moment he was referring to what had just passed between us, but clearly that wasn't the case; he put his hand on my shoulder and looked down at me, as at a friend: 'don't you think so?'

Now feeling uncertain I said: 'Like what?'

'That's the thing,' he said, 'language is so inadequate, we cannot express them: they are beyond the realm of meaning and words.'

'I believe that that may be so,' I said, believing indeed that that may be so, but still not fully grasping what he was getting at. Still, I felt it was time that we made a move, and so, putting my hand on the hand that he'd put on my shoulder and still speaking to him through the mirror, I said, hoping that this might settle his mind for a while and let him get on with the day: 'Well, I suppose whereof one cannot speak, thereof one must be silent.'

This seemed to satisfy him, and, feeling relieved, we left the apartment, glided down the stairs and strode up the avenue in the dappled shade of the afternoon sun, arm in arm, looking every bit not a couple of young lovers but a pair of old pals...

Epilogue

New York

1964-67

New Year 1964

The Ruby Dress. I call it the Ruby Dress, not because of its ruby color, but because when I put it on I *become* Ruby. Ruby Shoes, Ruby Lipstick, Ruby Hair. The hair is not ruby, it's a fabulous *electric* blue. It doesn't go with anything. The level to which it clashes is shocking, and that's the idea. The Ruby Stole: light green feathers setting off the hair; and the Ruby Nails. It's about minus four Fahrenheit outside, so if there's a line, people will die. 'That's not gonna be us,' Tommy insists, cause the guy who's put us on the guest list, is 'like the Queen of England: nightclub royalty, believe. You. Me.' Tommy stays cool most of the time, he doesn't really get excited, but you know he's impressed when his punctuation goes erratic. Still, that reminds me I was gonna use the Union Jack handbag, not the plain one, just to show him: I'm on message.

*

It takes me another half hour to do my eyelashes and then Tommy needs to swing by his dealer because he doesn't trust 'all the crap that'll be doing the rounds there', so by the time we get to the club, it's minutes before midnight and we just have enough time to get in some mojitos before the big countdown, and then *Auld Lang Syne*. That's when I catch her eyes and she's: *beautiful*. She's easily the most beautiful drag queen that I've ever seen. She doesn't even look like a drag queen, she's lean and delicate and extremely elegant; not garish at all, like most of us are, most of the time, even when we're not making an effort to be. She looks like a *lady*, which seems a little ironic. She catches me staring at her and sashays over: 'You must be Ruby,' holding out her hand with the kind of gesture that makes you think, am I supposed to I kiss it? I can't shake it, this is not the kind of hand that you *shake*. I bend forward and lift her long gloved fingers to my lips, but I don't let my lips touch her knuckles. She smiles. I'm stunned. I don't know how she knows who I am, I'm new on the circuit and actually quite shy, but she keeps beaming at me and says: 'I am Orlando, Tommy's friend, I got you in; you are technically my guest.' I don't know what to say, so I keep staring at her and she continues: 'You don't hold hands here, do you?' Now I'm completely lost: did I do the wrong thing? 'You just drape yourselves over whoever happens to be standing next to you: it does have its very own charm.'

*

I switch stares to Tommy, *uncomprehending.* What is this girl talking about? *'Auld Lang Syne,'* Tommy says: 'you hold hands for it, like this, in England.' Orlando corrects him: 'In fact, in Scotland you only cross arms on the last verse, when you sing: *"and there's a hand my trusty fiere! And gie's a hand o'thine..."* but very few people know this tradition, and fewer still honour it. As it happens, hardly anyone even knows the third verse...' She squeezes between us and demonstrates by offering us a hand each, crossing her arms in front of her, and then she gives us each a peck on the cheek and trills 'Happy New Year, both of you,' and, to me, 'love the bag, nice touch!' Then she disappears into the crazy melee. I'm not even sure what's just happened, but Tommy shrugs his shoulders and says: 'Told you.'

We drop a couple of Tommy's pills (that detour was a good call: they kick in straight away and the buzz is groovy and smooth) and I go in search for this Audrey-Hepburnesque vision that had appeared before me, because now I'm a little in love. This is unreal: *I'm a drag queen,* I don't fall for other drag queens, plus I'm here with Tommy, and we don't play around (much). But she's *exquisite.* I find her perched on a sofa talking to a guy wearing shades. She sees me and beckons me over. 'Ruby, darling, meet Andy, he's a very talented artist.' The guy with the shades is so softly spoken, I can't catch a word of what he's saying, but then he doesn't say much anyway, he just smiles at me sweetly, and I'm now high on speed so I don't really care. Tommy comes over and Orlando excuses herself by giving the artist guy a peck on the cheek too, just as she'd given us, and mouths in his ear: 'Happy New Year: make it *special...*' The artist guy stays seated with his inscrutable expression half obscured by those sunglasses, but he seems happy enough there, while Orlando joins us and puts a cigarette on her filter, gets Tommy to light it for her and dances a little dance all by herself, with the artist guy watching.

Tuesday, April 21st – 6 p.m.

Somebody arrives at our Greenwich Village apartment wearing a dark suit and a dark tie and sharp shoes, and I don't even recognise him because he's got a haircut like one of the Beatles—who by the way are now on spots *one to five* in the US singles chart, they are *all over the place;* what is that all about?—and I think I might still be hallucinating from all the acid I'd been taking over the weekend, either that or John Lennon has just popped round for coffee, but this one's much better looking, and when he opens his mouth and that soft, lilting voice comes out with, 'Ruby, darling, where's Tommy, I have some *magnificent* news, but we have to get our skates on,' do I get it's Orlando. 'Tommy's not here right now, but come in, what's the news?' Orlando makes straight for the fridge and helps himself to some ice cubes and a shot of vodka from the kitchen cupboard: 'We are going to Andy's first public show at the Factory.'

Friday, April 24th

It's taken me a couple of days to get over it. Seriously: either that man is a complete genius, or I have to stop taking drugs immediately, or both. Orlando takes us Midtown to this studio on East 47th, and to me it looks pretty much like we're never going to get in: there are people waiting round the block, but Orlando ushers us right through and up six floors in a jam-packed elevator, and suddenly we're in this huge space which is decked out in silver foil with silver paint on the walls, music blaring out from speakers everywhere and some kind of light show going on, and the room is filled with... grocery boxes. Just the kind of boxes you'd find in a supermarket or warehouse that would have Brillo pads in them, or tomato juice or whatever, but they don't, they're made of wood and printed on, so I say to Orlando, 'what the hell is this?' and he laughs and says: 'they're *sculptures!*'

The crowd is astonishing: you've got just about everybody here that matters, and I think I at one point *literally* bump into Michael Caine of all people, I don't know what he's doing in town, and then in the middle of it all you've got this Andy Warhol character playing host, smiling benignly at people and welcoming them to his show. To my utter surprise he remembers me, or at least he pretends to, but then unlike Orlando, who hasn't changed out of his suit, I'm here in full Ruby regalia, and Andy says I need to come back as he's now making movies. I tell him I'd love to be in one of his movies but I'm not really an actor, and he says that's just perfect because I'm 'so *beautiful!...*' I don't know what to make of it all, but on the way out I overhear someone say to someone else who is staggering down the stairs, trying not to fall over: 'I think the Sixties have just begun.'

Friday, June 12th

Orlando and I have been going back to the Factory two or three times a week now for over a month, sometimes daily. I keep expecting Tommy to get jealous, but he's got himself a steady job now and has gotten really quite respectable, so he hasn't got any time anyway and he doesn't seem to mind at all; if anything he seems happy for me to have someone to hang out with. The Factory is an amazing place. People come and go all the time, drag queens, freaks, artists, hustlers, writers, models, and practically every day somebody famous comes in. It seems everybody and anybody who comes to New York is paying a visit to the Factory. There are movie stars like Dennis Hopper and rock stars like David Bowie and then there are people like Baby Jane Holzer and Gerard Malanga who aren't really stars at all but Andy calls them 'Superstars' anyway because he reckons that soon everybody "will be famous for fifteen minutes," and there are certainly a lot of people hanging out here who are dying for their fifteen minutes of fame.

*

A few weeks ago we both made a short film portrait each with Andy. He calls them Screen Tests, but they're not really screen tests at all, because they don't lead to anything else, they're just experiments in their own right. The setup is really simple: Andy positions the camera and you sit down in front of it and once he's happy with the frame, he starts recording and walks away. The film lasts as long as the film in the cartridge, which is nearly three minutes, and you're on your own. Orlando seemed comfortable. He decided to wear neither drag nor normal clothes but kind of a period shirt that looked like something from Elizabethan England, and then he had me put some make-up on him, very subtle, very androgynous, very sexy. Then he just sat there and looked into the camera, and did nothing at all. I found it hard. I'd come as Ruby – I always come as Ruby, the Factory is one of the few places where I can be at home just as I am when I'm Ruby, I don't even have to put on an act anymore, I can just be there. But sitting in front of a camera for three minutes is tough, you feel tempted to start mugging at the lens doing stuff and you think how can anyone find this interesting. But it is interesting. When you watch it back you realize: you can watch a face forever. And the less somebody does, in a way the more interesting it becomes.

This week, we continued work on *Kiss,* which Andy started last year. The principle is exactly the same: a couple—doesn't matter in what configuration—kiss and Andy films it. On this occasion, Gerard was kissing Mark Lancaster. I was kind of hoping Andy would ask Orlando and me to kiss for him too, but he didn't, and I wasn't going to suggest it because I didn't want to come across too pushy with Orlando...

Andy's movies are all kind of cool and weird at the same time. Earlier in the year, he made *Sleep.* It's literally just him filming his boyfriend John, while he's asleep. For hours. And *Blowjob,* where he keeps the camera not where you'd expect but on the guy's face. The reason I love these movies is not just because they're simple, but because he slows them down: he shoots them at a normal 24 frames per second, but then when he projects them he shows them at 16 frames a second, which is a third slower and just makes them look mesmerizing.

Sunday, July 19th

Things really kicked off in Harlem last night and there are reports of many injured and also some dead. Tommy is worried about me because I've been crying since Thursday. It's just too awful: the shooting of James Powell has set us back, I don't know, thirty years. Martin Luther King has again called for restraint and peaceful, non-violent protests, but tensions are so high now, it fills me with dread and despair. Orlando is very sweet, he tries to comfort me by saying things like: 'the struggle will be worth it,' and 'we shall, in fact, overcome,' but I find it hard to believe and whenever he holds me I cry even more. My brothers and sisters are being shot down and beaten up and then blamed for their anger at a time when we are still so racially divided that most people just don't have a chance: I don't understand it. I kind of wish I could get out of town for a bit, New York can be just too intense...

Wednesday, October 28th

Poor little Freddy. He said he was going to do this, but nobody believed him, because when somebody says, come round to mine, I'm having a party and I'll be jumping off the roof, you don't think, yeah sure, that's *exactly* what you're gonna be doing. We were at Di's at the time, just chilling, talking, smoking, and he wanted to borrow an LP or something, I wasn't paying that much attention to be honest. He said, come over, it'll be a happening. We kind of laughed, we thought it was funny. But the speed really does something to people. I've said this to Billy at the Factory, 'you gotta be careful with these drugs, man, they change people,' and he smiled and said, 'yes, sure, that's what they do.'

Then last night Freddy went round to his friend, Johnny Dodd's, and he says, 'I'm gonna have a bath,' so he goes and has his bath and then he puts on a record, the Coronation Mass by Mozart. And he dances, high as a kite, and when the *Sanctus* comes on, he dances right out of the window. But he doesn't just dance, it's not like: oh, I just happen to be dancing out of the window; he jumped, he took a leap. He killed himself. And I don't think anybody knows why. He was beautiful. And kind. And yeah, maybe there was a dark side, I don't know, isn't there always?

Saturday, November 7th

Thursday Orlando and I went to Freddy's funeral service at Judson Memorial Church in Washington Square. Everybody was there, everybody was crying. Everybody is sad. Well, I'm not sure Andy is really sad. It's kind of disturbing, he told one of his friends, Peter I think, that it was a shame nobody was there with a camera to film it when Freddy jumped. Peter was furious. I'm furious too, it's a heartless thing to say, even if you're the coolest artist on the planet. I think a lot of people are angry with Andy, he doesn't seem to care. Maybe he can't, maybe he's too absorbed in his own world. Maybe we all are too absorbed in our own worlds. Maybe we're all too absorbed in *his* world. Orlando sure seems to think so. He's quite wary of it all, I think. Fascinated, yes, but wary. And if you see what's going down at the Factory, you understand why: there's fabulous stuff happening, don't get me wrong, during the summer he made these 40 X 40 inch silk screen prints of Marilyn, and they're fabulous. They capture everything. That's what he does, he captures everything. But he doesn't connect. Orlando says he's taking the Christopher Isherwood principle to another level. I didn't know who Christopher Isherwood was, so Orlando explained he's the guy who went to Berlin and wrote the book on which the Broadway play *I Am a Camera* is based. 'This idea,' Orlando goes, 'of just being the observer, of capturing everything, of being completely disengaged and objective but actually creating the culture in doing so.' Orlando thinks Isherwood was ahead of his time but Andy is exactly of his time. 'Andy *is* New York today,' says Orlando, 'he's worked it out for himself and he's orchestrating a microcosm of everything that makes New York what it is in his Factory. It's brilliant, and it's shocking and it's extremely creative and it's also very destructive.' I've never heard Orlando talk like that. He's been very quiet and very serious lately. I haven't seen his mildly flamboyant, delicate charm at all recently, when I come to think of it. It bothers me.

Sunday, November 22nd

Andy's new show opened at the Castelli Gallery: flowers. They're cool. Kind of. They're not exactly revolutionary, but they're very Andy. He's dedicated a white flower to Freddy. Which is nice...

Tuesday, December 8th

Andy has won an independent filmmakers award. Not everybody is thrilled. I actually am; though I reckon they should have cited *Blowjob* too, not just *Sleep, Haircut, Kiss* and the others, but I guess they weren't quite brave enough. Some people are positively angry, and I guess if you've been a serious filmmaker for the last ten years, beavering away at making indie movies and never getting much recognition and then along comes Andy Warhol getting an award for pointing a camera, that must be pretty annoying. But it was a good night and everybody at the Factory seems a lot happier. Andy was handing out fruit to his 'Superstars' as 'awards'. He does have a sense of humor about it all...

To deal with last night's hangover, Orlando awarded us both with the best Bloody Mary I've ever had mixed for me. The more time I spend with him, the more I like him. I wonder has he abandoned being a drag queen altogether, so I ask him, and I realize I've not really asked him anything about himself at all, not ever, I don't think, and so I also ask him what brings him to New York and what his plans are. I'm a bit scared I'm probing too hard, because I also realize, I've gone into the 'I don't want to push my luck with this guy, but maybe I want more from him, but I also don't want to lose what I've got of him now' phase, and I always get that phase so catastrophically wrong.

Orlando says he was just travelling and having a look around; he'd wanted to go to Tokyo, but remembered he couldn't really speak Japanese. I said, 'what do you mean, "really"?' – 'Well, it's not a big problem,' he thought at first, 'I've learnt other languages before,' but then he reckoned it would be 'as interesting seeing the world come together in one place where he was already familiar with the idiom, as going everywhere and starting from scratch.' As so often I don't really understand what he means, though I'm kind of used to that now. The drag thing he says was just 'playing around'. This makes me a little uneasy. I know for a lot of people drag queens are figures of fun. Then he asks me whether I actually consider myself to be a transgender person. I shrug, I don't know. I don't think so, but I don't really know what I am. I don't know anything at the moment, I'm this great big six foot three black guy from the Bronx and I'm mixing with people I've never mixed with before and I'm learning stuff that I've never imagined and I'm having my heart peeled open by this tender, intelligent, *different* young guy who seems to be coming from everywhere and nowhere at the same time... – The Bloody Marys appear to be doing a great job, I'm getting sentimental. 'So did you actually go to Tokyo?' – 'Oh no, I didn't. This time, I was wise before the event.' I didn't know what that meant either, but I leant forward to kiss him and he kissed me back. This was the first time. We've known each other for nearly a year now, and we've never come as close as this, even to kissing. Sure, for the first six months or so I was technically seeing Tommy, but once you've been to the Factory, or some of the parties in some of the clubs, or to any of the people's houses: people don't hesitate to kiss. They don't hesitate to do anything. You know the words that spring to mind here but I don't want anyone who ever reads this to feel like they're having to imagine ********* everywhere so I'll just leave it to your imagination. Still: we're talking *orgies* here, right. Not so with Orlando...

Sunday, March 21st, 1965

There is a new beauty in town and she captivates everybody. Andy is smitten. Even Orlando seems taken with her. Her name's Edie and she's almost exactly what Orlando would be if he were in fact a woman. 'It's most disconcerting,' he admits. She's like 22, drives around town in a Mercedes-Benz and parties with the kind of style other girls can't even muster the imagination to dream of. At the party for the *Life Magazine* spread, Orlando looked at her and then turned around to me and said: 'She's lost two of her brothers too, you know, isn't that sad?' And he did have a real sadness in his eyes, as if he were mourning them for her, and I said: 'Have you lost two brothers?' He snapped out of it and gave me a tired little smile: 'Not me, a friend...'

Sunday, June 20th

Went to the premiere last night of *Poor Little Rich Girl* in which Edie Sedgwick effectively stars as herself. She's gorgeous, there's no taking that away from her. Orlando says she 'radiates precisely the loss of self that a culture completely fixated on an external expression of the ego makes inevitable.' He no longer feels that comfortable being around the Factory set and he is not the only one. Several of the regulars have drifted away or fallen by the wayside, or simply died. The lifestyle is taking its toll. Somebody said, and I don't think it was the speed talking, 'he really sucks you dry, Drella.' Drella is Andy's nickname: Dracula/Cinderella. Orlando calls it 'curiously apt.'

Thursday, December 16th

Not since he first started working with Edie have I seen Andy so excited. He went to *Bizarre* last night and he says he's found the band he's been looking for. I frankly didn't know he was looking for a band, but I guess that's what makes Andy special: he really doesn't stop at anything, he just does whatever the hell he likes. Maybe that's at the end of the day what really makes an artist: to actually not give a damn. They're called The Velvet Underground. Orlando says, 'if Andy takes them on as their manager, then they might just do to music what he's done to art.' Orlando hasn't even heard them yet...

Sunday, April 10th, 1966 – 3 p.m.

Oh wow. That was so crazy, and so amazing and so out there and so everything that you'd want from a happening, I'm still buzzing and it's two days later. Orlando is still asleep. I need some vegetable juice or something but I'm hoping the typewriter will wake him up, because I don't want to go out for breakfast on my own. So that was *The Exploding Plastic Inevitable* upstairs at the Dom. Seriously: I don't even know where to begin. Obviously, The Velvet Underground, in shades on stage; then Andy up on the balcony like a god or something looking down on his creation, and his film being projected on the band and these lights and *the drugs.* There are people going round literally injecting audience members with speed, right through their clothes. I have never seen so many people so off their faces have such a wild experience, I don't even know if I can go back there. Hedonism? This isn't even an ism any more this is just *abandon.*

Monday, 26th June 1967

Darling Ruby

I so wish you could have seen this, it would have cheered your gentle giant heart. They connected the whole world together in one single television broadcast via satellite: it was truly remarkable. Our little globe is becoming ever so small, and how magnificent is it, is it not?, that it should be possible to have the peoples of many nations experience the same spectacle, the same sensations, perhaps even the same emotions, at exactly the same time. You see, there is hope, like we said. I so wish you could have seen it and I so wish I could have you near me and look up into those dark brown twinkling eyes of yours. I do miss you terribly. I haven't had the stomach to write anything at all, no poetry, no diary, no letters, just nothing, since I found you, on the big red sofa, lying there as if you were taking a nap. I so wish I didn't have to just find you, I so wish I could have been there, called an ambulance, done something, done anything at all, but that's the insidious nature of these substances, I suppose; they strike without warning. Was there no warning? I so wish I had listened to the warnings, I feel so very culpable. But aren't we all? Aren't we all just trying to make something of it, as best we can? There are extraordinary things happening all over the world now; and everybody seems to be going to San Francisco. I think I shall go there too. I have no idea what I might be doing there or how I shall ever not feel this terrible loss and this terrible fondness I have for you. My darling Ruby, I wish you could come with me. And how I wish you could have seen this thing yesterday. They did segments from a dozen countries or so. The last one came from London. You would have so very much liked it: The Beatles closed the show with a new song they wrote especially for this Our World broadcast. It is called All You Need Is Love.

Peace, You Beautiful Human Being, Peace
Orlando

Coda

i am orlando

breathless
at the bacchanal
bewitched, senses
submerged, my image
mirrored, my mind
magicked, my emotions
modulated
magnified
unmoderated and maybe
immodest, myself
multiplied:

masked dancer at the carnival
bald bearded lady, fashionista
beehive diva, torch song bearer of my soul
pole-dancing scientist
shop floor assistant checking out
the other side, experimenter, part-time genius
moustachioed hipster sophist nerd geek self-inventor and

bespectacled spectator
taking in, in-
haling, hailing without praise or
condemnation
participant observer, being-done-to
doer

all exposed

the pushing
to the fore, persistent rushing shoreward of
wave upon wave:
the daily deluge of disaster
wilfully
constructed, or else
wantonly permitted to occur and then
dispersed
with breathless kick and fury
horned-up with excitement
round the clock
catastrophe porn paired with power penetration to the
brain: every
second someone selling something
a tsunami of musthave dispensables

then news again the weather breaking down ten thousand
perish in a flood

security alert
three men arrested at the airport
one who fled
soft-spoken leaker of state secrets swears allegiance to
the people; people
protest
the police, the army
bullets rifles hand grenades, ex-
superpower eyeing up her neighbours' territories, boundaries
unkept, unrecognised, rendered irrelevant
space probe touchdown on the comet, cheers and champagne at
base, break through
the tunnel, high speed trains
dark matter and dark energy
the murder of the messengers
a million on the streets in solidarity, fighters
of and for freedom feeling pain, offenders
in each other's eyes – our
tears all taste the same

a smartphone
with an app the university that taps into the global lecture hall
a telescope array across a mountain table peering deep into
the origin of
time, and
cupcakes
talent shows, made-up

realities
downloads, stolen
identities and
printed body parts
milestones in mending memories, the
tantalising likelihood that we are not alone
sandcastles made of stars, stars
made of frivolities
cat videos
and piles
and piles
of rubbish

rejects
refugees
residents of uncertainty, nomads by
adverse conditions, the
collateral of calamity
unwanted
unloved, un-
understood
disowned dishonoured dismissed dishevelled, dis-
affected
indistinct
in the morass
of mass
morbidity, in-

visible

flashes of inspiration
fascinations
colours, glitter
decadences
balls: exuberances
festivals and
congregations, close
communions
travel at the speed of sound, lightspeed
communication
instantaneous pools of
commonality
the vibe and exultation, the
euphoria
the sharpwit razor of precision, the
ingeniousness
the shared experience
the climactic joy, the
sacred orgasm of
life

i rest
i pause

i meditate, i am
orlando
i reflect

i have no solution, there are no solutions
i have no anger: anger is void, i
ease
i learn
i think
i offer

silence

i
become
the citizen
and i see sparks of wisdom and then once again i laugh
i love
i give
i take
i lose myself
i win
i love again, i want and want not and want not to want, i
realise
i am a part of it: i am

a part
of everything, every
thing
is part of me

i am the gods
i am the universe
i am the energy
i am the code
i am the probability
i am the failure and the hope and the despair
i am the triumph
of existence

that is what i am:
i
am

orlando

www.ingramcontent.com/pod-product-compliance
Ingram Content Group UK Ltd.
Pitfield, Milton Keynes, MK11 3LW, UK
UKHW040004200726
13854UKWH00001B/30

9 781638 219996